DEPOT DORA

STOLEN MASTERPIECES AND HIDDEN TREASURES

CY VAUGHN

Depot Dora: Stolen Masterpieces and Hidden Treasures

Published by Wheatmark®
1760 East River Road, Suite 145
Tucson, Arizona 85718 USA
www.wheatmark.com

ISBN: 978-1-62787-415-1 (paperback)
ISBN: 978-1-62787-416-8 (ebook)
LCCN: 2016938136

Note: The symbol used on the chapter pages of 31–33 is the Austrian Coat of Arms.

For my children: Vicki Vaughn Roden, RN; Cecil Vaughn III, MD; Katherine Vaughn Fielder, PhD; Michael Vaughn, Esq; Paul Vaughn, MD; and Barbara Vaughn, their mother.

ACKNOWLEDGMENTS

Credit is due the original Operation Ebensburg crew: the leader, Albrecht Gaiswinkler; Karl Standhartinger; Karl Litzer; and Josef Grafl. Gaiswinkler wrote the first book describing their mission: *Sprung in die Freiheit (Leap Into Freedom) 1945.*

My thanks to university Professor Dr. Ernst Wolner, MD, Chairman of the Bilroth Second Surgical Unit, University of Vienna Hospital, who first told me of the saga of the Altaussee Salt Mine. My idea for *Depot Dora* was born as I stood on wooden scaffolding in the Mineral Cabinet where the Nazis stored the stolen art.

My heartfelt thanks to Kaye, my wife and first reader, whose artistic eye and feeling for the story helped shape the plot points and stylistic design of *Depot Dora.*

Kudos to Lori Leavitt, senior project manager, and all the staff at Wheatmark Publishing. Their professional advice and editing honed and focused the narrative.

I am indebted to officials of the salt mine and Altaussee villagers who shared their emotional memories of this tragic era.

AUTHOR'S NOTE

Depot Dora is based on a heroic British World War II mission: Operation Ebensburg. In June 1944, Austrian patriot Albrecht Gaiswinkler defected from the Wehrmacht (German Army) to the Maquis (French Resistance). The British Special Operations Executive (SOE) called him to London to train as a covert agent. On April 8, 1945, he parachuted into the Altaussee area and quickly organized a large force of Austrian Resistance fighters. They captured a number of high-ranking Nazi officers, including Ernst Kaltenbrunner, who were retreating to their alpine redoubt in the forest above Altaussee.

Nazi thieves stored the world's largest treasure trove of art masterpieces in Depot Dora, Hitler's code name for the salt mine at Altaussee. Hitler issued his Nero's decree, ordering destruction of the salt mine and its precious contents.

Gaiswinkler and the Austrian Resistance blew up the mine entrance, saving the art inside, including the *Mona Lisa*.

The French government and Louvre officials deny that the *Mona Lisa* was ever in Nazi hands. Records of the SOE, however, confirm that da Vinci's masterpiece was indeed in Depot Dora and was saved along with the rest of the art.

In 1986 I interviewed Josef Grafl, radio operator for Operation Ebensburg, at his home in Bad Aussee. A man of short stature, he welcomed me. "Come in, would you like a beer?"

Many of the events of Depot Dora are attributed to this Austrian hero. He did complain that his country "never paid us, not even a new suit of clothes. Friends in my village did not like my helping the English. When I walked into a bar the talking stopped, and they said, 'Here is the Englander.'" He and Gaiswinkler had little to do with each other after the war, although they were neighbors.

The image of a German swastika appears at the top of each page of a new chapter. However the first pages of chapters 31, 32, and 33 are headed by an image of the Austrian Coat of Arms, signifying regained Austrian freedom.

PROLOGUE

Altaussee, Austria

December 10, 1944. Heavily armed Nazi convoys delivered eight coffin-sized wooden crates to Depot Dora, Hitler's code name for the salt mine at Altaussee, Austria. The arduous 360-kilometer trip from Neuschwanstein Castle over mountainous, icy roads had been simple compared to the steep grade of the snow-covered mud track leading up to the salt mine.

Once there, the Wehrmacht soldiers unloaded the crates onto small motor-driven carts on a narrow-gauge railroad that took them deep into the multichambered mine.

The crates were deposited into the Mineral Cabinet, a cavernous rock-walled room lined on all sides by lumber scaffolding that held smaller crates of Nazi-confiscated masterpieces from museums, cathedrals, and mansions all over Europe. Near the end of World War II, a total of 6,577 masterpieces, including the *Mona Lisa*, were saved by an Austrian patriot, Lucas Brunn.

1

Altaussee, Austria
December 24, 1944

Lucas Brunn crept into the nave of the dimly lit St. Michael's Catholic Church, crossed himself, and sat down in the last row of straight-backed pews made of Austrian pine.

To his left, a small Christmas tree of alpine fir, its lights darkened, stood atop a wooden table. Wondering why Father Messmer had asked him to come, he glanced at his watch, checked the door, and after four minutes walked to the aisle to his right. He pulled back the red velvet curtain of the confessional and stepped in. Soft amber light glowed through the oak latticework screen. He heard the tapping of Father Messmer's cane and, as he leaned closer, the throaty growl of Donner, his German Shepherd.

Lucas knelt on the prie-dieu. "Forgive me, Father, for I have sinned."

"We have no time, Lucas," the priest whispered. "Listen carefully to what I'm going to tell you. First, your father knows and approves of your being here."

"Where is my father?"

"He is in a special meeting."

"On Christmas Eve? What meeting?"

"Do you know that your father is in the Austrian Resistance? He is meeting with them now."

Lucas said nothing.

"You must answer."

"He told me to never discuss it."

"My son, you must put the cause of the Resistance ahead—"

"What are we talking about?"

"Do not be impatient with a man of God." Silence engulfed them for a moment, and Father Messmer continued. "I will explain. Nazi convoys have been delivering large wooden crates to the salt mine. We fear that they may contain explosives, gold, or stolen art. For years they have been looting masterpieces from museums, churches, castles, and wealthy families."

"Why are you telling me this?"

"A Resistance courier from the meeting arrived an hour ago with this message: the Austrian Resistance Committee needs someone to go into the mine and find out what is in the crates. They have selected you for this mission."

"I'm not in the Resistance."

"You are now. Your father nominated you."

Lucas paused, laced his fingers, and took a deep breath. "This is unbelievable. For the past year, since the Nazis Aryanized der Medizinische Universität Wien—"

"The Vienna Medical School . . . controlled by Nazis?"

"I thought you knew. They allow only students who have German birth certificates to study there. They limit studies to trauma and caring for wounded soldiers. They are really only training army medics."

"I am so saddened to learn of this."

"Since I left school, I've tried to join the Resistance, but Father forbade it. And now he does this, without asking me? Incredible. Why would he change his mind? Why didn't he tell me?"

"I am sorry that your career has been interrupted, but all of our lives may be forever changed and, if we do not resist, perhaps lost."

"I hate the Nazis for what they've done to our homeland, and I would do anything for Austria." Lucas leaned forward and buried his face in his hands. His heart raced. "Why me, Father? I could be captured or killed. Sure, I'm eager to fight the Nazis, but I don't know how to be a spy. An injury to my hands could end my dream of being a surgeon."

"We could discuss this for hours, but the question of the moment is this: are you willing to help Austria fight the Nazis?"

"I don't know, Father. I'm so afraid I'll fail and—"

"Hear me out, Lucas. The committee has a plan. The miners have requested a priest to bless them in St. Barbara's Chapel. You will go disguised as a priest. After the blessing you will make your way to the Mineral Cabinet, where the cases are stored. Open one crate, find out what's inside, and leave. That is all."

"All? I can't act like a priest, and just how can I get away after the blessing and find the Mineral Cabinet? Madness."

"Your father wants you to go, because this mission is vital to the cause, and the committee selected you because of your strength and athleticism."

"That's not fair."

"My son, in these times nothing is fair."

"Abel will be here tomorrow. He'll go with me. I know he will. He's a street fighter. He can do this mission. We've been like brothers since first grade."

Father Messmer sat back and folded his hands. "Abel Graf is being hunted by the Gestapo."

"Why?"

"He was part of a plot to assassinate a Gestapo agent in Graz. The plot failed. Abel was injured, but he escaped. He has been here for two days. He serves on the committee and volunteered to go with you, but this must be a solo mission. Two spies are more likely to be discovered than one. Now, let's proceed."

The priest opened the screen and handed Lucas folded documents. "Here are your papers. You are Father Stefan Bauder from Bad Aussee, there to say a prayer for the miners in St. Barbara's Chapel."

Lucas glanced at the papers and looked up at Father Messmer. He wore a white clerical gown and cap with protruding wisps of silver hair. Round silver-rimmed glasses sat low on his pug nose. He had a round face with cherry-red cheeks that reminded Lucas of St. Nicholas.

"Father Bauder has black hair."

"Your hat is large and will cover your hair. Do not take it off. I've written a short prayer for you. Memorize it and destroy the paper. Mine officials are expecting you. After the ceremony ask them if you might spend some time alone in the chapel for prayers. Should they agree, wait until everyone leaves and make your way to the Mineral Cabinet. If they insist on seeing you out, the mission is aborted. Do you understand?"

"Aborted? Strange word for a priest."

"Listen to me," the padre said with a note of exasperation in his voice. "Only one miner knows of the plan. After the ceremony he will come to you. Do not search for him. He will give you a headlamp and a map with directions. Your job is to discover the contents of one large crate. Nothing more. Once you have done that, leave. Remember: pray, open crate, leave."

"I wish Abel could go with me. He's always protected me. I'm afraid, Father."

The priest paused and handed Lucas a scabbard. "Here's a hunting knife. Use it only in a life-or-death situation."

"I don't know how to use a knife. I wouldn't kill a bird."

The priest sighed. "There is a brown paper bag next to the prie-dieu. In it are black horn-rimmed glasses, a flashlight, clerical clothes, a small toolbox, and black shoes. You must wear the black shoes. I heard your shoes squeak when you came in the confessional. Did you bring extra clothes as I asked?"

"I did."

"Good. Put the clerical clothes on, place the clothes you are wearing in the bag, and leave the bag on the floor. After you change, be sure to insert the white Roman collar."

Lucas chuckled. "Do you think I'll make a handsome priest, Father?" Lucas, standing just shy of six feet and weighing one hundred and seventy pounds , was indeed handsome. Many of the girls thought he resembled Van Johnson, the American movie idol. He stood tall and military straight with a shock of wheat-colored hair, a spray of freckles across the bridge of his nose, and happy eyes, blue as the Mediterranean.

"No jokes now, Lucas. Otto will meet you at the side door and drive you to the road leading up to the mine. You will have to walk from there. After the mission, when you come out of the mine"—the priest paused and squeezed Lucas's forearm—"try to act as normal as possible. Walk past the point where Otto dropped you off, go to the right, and find the entrance gate to the motor vehicle repair yard. He will be parked near there and flash his headlights twice. Go to him, and he'll bring you back to the church." He paused. "That's it."

Lucas opened the paper bag and dressed as instructed. As he opened the confessional curtain to leave, he heard Father Messmer whisper, "Go with God, my son."

2

Lucas stepped from the church and looked toward the parking area. A black Opel, its lights switched off and engine idling, stood nearby. He climbed into the front seat, and Otto said, "And how are you this fine evening, Father?"

Lucas said nothing and nodded for Otto to drive. They rumbled along dark, deserted Kirchestrasse, a gravel road that in former years had been alive on Christmas Eve with Yuletide revelers, music, and glittering Christmas lights. This year, though, no mountain folk, singing all the way, had trekked into the village. There had been no gaiety and *frohe Weihnachten* (Merry Christmas) since the Anschluss, only darkness, with blackout curtains drawn shut on houses choked with fear. A gibbous moon hung above rows of cottages with empty flower boxes and smoke curling from chimneys, pasting white apostrophes onto a black sky.

It began to snow as they turned onto Hauptstrasse and drove past the village square. Lucas remembered past years when there had been a giant Christmas tree decorated with gold and silver ornaments. On the far side of the square, Hotel Seevilla's bright lights illuminated a giant swastika.

They left the village on Salzburgerstrasse and headed toward the salt mine. Lucas glanced at Otto, who was intent on his driving. He knew little about this short, chubby man other than he was the church janitor, handyman, chauffeur, and assistant to the priest. And now he was about to entrust his life to him. He opened the note with the prayer, read it twice using a small flashlight, tore it into small pieces, and let them fly out of the window.

His mind flashed to his father. *Why would he do this? My mother's death at my birth had cast an impenetrable barrier between us. I tried to talk to the man, and when I grew older, I told him that I loved him. But I've never heard those words from my father. Has he sent me on this mission with sinister intent? My God. I don't want to die.*

They drove up the steep grade of Lichtersberggasse, a narrow gravel ribbon weaving through the encroaching forest. Just beyond a wooden fence, they rattled to a stop at a small side trail. Otto set the brake and put his hand on Lucas's shoulder and said, *"Gute Reise."* Safe journey.

Lucas nodded and got out, and as he closed the door, the Opel slipped into the darkness. Rifts of moonlight washed through the bare limbs of giant elms, casting an eerie, shadowy mosaic on the snow-covered muddy trail leading up to the mine, der Sternburg Haus.

Around the first turn of the trail, Lucas gasped as a German soldier stepped from a guard shack and leveled his rifle. Wide-eyed, he raised his hands.

"Bitte, Papier." Papers, please.

Still as a stone, Lucas slowly lowered his arms and reached toward his cape pocket.

The guard jerked his rifle to eye level. "Slowly, Father."

Lucas nodded, carefully removed his identity papers between his right thumb and index finger, and handed them to the guard.

The young Nazi stood as tall as Lucas. Tufts of blond hair sprouted below his helmet, and his ferretlike face was dominated by bushy eyebrows over eyes that were too close together and a small nose. His leather-gloved hands were as strong and wide as boat oars. Lucas guessed he was a farm boy.

The Nazi focused his flashlight on the forged identity papers, worn with a crease distorting his picture. He read the name and guided his flashlight onto Lucas's face. He studied the eyes and glanced back at the picture.

Lucas raised his eyes to the moon and prayed: must not take my hat off.

"Ah, Father Bauder, I also come from St. Polten."

Lucas raised his hand to shade his eyes from the blinding light. "Yes, well, you are fortunate to have the opportunity to serve the Reich so near to your home. That is good. What is your name, my son?"

Still looking at the papers, he replied, "Ernst. My family comes from Niedling. Do you know it?"

The snowfall intensified, large flakes glistening in the flashlight's beam.

Lucas fought for calm. "Of course, great farm country . . . Niedling." He nodded toward the mine. "I'm afraid I'm late. They're waiting for me to bless the miners in St. Barbara's Chapel."

The soldier stared again at the papers for what seemed an eternity and handed them to Lucas. "Come into the guard shack. I must take your picture."

Lucas's heart pounded as he followed the guard, who walked to a desk and removed a camera from a drawer.

"That's quite a camera you have there," Lucas said, his voice cracking.

"Yes, it is a Leica Luftwaffe two, the best. Herr Goering confiscated them for his pilots. This one came from a crashed Messerschmitt near Salzburg."

The guard aimed the camera, and Lucas posed, tilting his head a bit and hoping the flash reflection from his glasses might blur his facial characteristics. He slammed his eyelids shut as the flash exploded.

The guard replaced the camera in the drawer and stared at Lucas. "You are very young. How long have you been a priest?"

"Only six months. I've been assigned my first parish in Bad Aussee."

Lucas wondered if the guard could hear his heart pounding.

They walked out of the shack, and the guard raised the white crossbar. "Say a prayer for lonely guards, Father."

Lucas raised his right hand. "Bless you, my son."

He eased past the guard and continued the climb toward the salt mine entrance. His mind raced. Had Father Messmer and his father known there would be a photograph? Out of sight of the guard, he stopped and leaned on the trunk of an elm to catch his breath in the thin mountain air. He whispered the prayer to himself and looked down at the village. Lights were blacked out, as they had been for three years. Most villagers thought this was unnecessary. Surely their alpine Eden was too small and remote to be attacked by American bombing raids.

Gathering layers of fog floated across the road like strung-out cotton candy. He squinted toward the stone building, a sinister white dinosaur bathed in an orange glow from lights framing the mine entrance.

No one knew what was in the crates, but the Nazis must be up to something. He whispered his mission to himself. "Pray, open crate, leave."

As he started up the trail, he wondered if he was climbing a gallows.

3

Lucas stepped across narrow-gauge rails and took a stone walkway into the mine. A guard stopped him, checked his papers, and searched him. He pointed and said, "Take the stairs up and enter the first room on the left."

Lucas climbed the steps and entered a room with a cement floor and white stucco walls, barren except for a photo of der Führer. A Nazi flag drooped in a corner. He sat at a wooden desk with four chairs.

Voices approached in the hallway. A quiet voice said, "The conditions in the mine are ideal for storing art: constant temperature and humidity . . . perfect."

A louder voice responded, "I agree, but the name of the mine is absurd. Do you know what it means?"

"Nothing certain, but I've heard rumors. Several years ago, before Eva Braun, Hitler named it after one of his paramours. It's his code name for the mine: Depot Dora."

The loud voice said, "Ah so. Shall we go in?" He knocked on the door. "Father, are you there?"

"Yes. Please come in."

The two men entered; one was slight of build with round

gold-rimmed glasses and graying black hair; the other was a bald-headed giant who blinked repeatedly.

The bald one said, "Father, I am Herr Heinrich Schulz, director of mines in Oberdonau; this is Herr Karl Maier, a frequent visitor to our village. He is on holiday from his position as art restorer of the Bavarian State Museum in Munich." Schulz removed a folded sheet of paper from his coat pocket and read as he continued. "Herr Maier, may I introduce Father Stefan Bauder. He is our guest from Bad Aussee and comes for a small ceremony to bless the miners."

Lucas raised his right hand in greeting.

Schulz said, "Come, they are waiting for us in the chapel."

They made their way through a heavy iron door into a widened space with open cabinets full of folded white canvas jumpsuits.

Schulz said, "Father, we must wear these protective suits for our journey." They put them on and walked to waiting flatbed cars. Schultz bowed mockingly and gestured toward the cars. "They are called *Hunde*."

"Ah, dogs?" Lucas said, forcing a chuckle.

"The miners have great imaginations."

The cars were two by five meters and pulled by a gasoline engine with a running board on either side of the engineer's platform. Schulz and Maier climbed into a car facing each other. With Schulz's girth there was no room for a third person.

Lucas, riding alone, had trouble folding his long legs into the compartment. He nodded to his engineer, the engine coughed to life, and they chugged into a dark tunnel. Lucas ducked and folded his arms to avoid shining, jagged stalactites of green, purple, and red-colored salt rock protruding from the ceiling and wall. Flickering lamps lighted the narrow rails as they rattled forward. They rode for ten minutes, got off, and walked along a passageway leading to an oval-shaped room with walls of red sandstone. A curved altar fronted a large, brightly colored picture of the patron, Saint Barbara. The miners believed that she protected them. The soft blue lighting of the stone behind the picture bestowed a holy iridescence on the chapel.

A gaggle of miners stood before the altar. They were dwarf-like men dressed in green lederhosen, long white socks, and black braces over green woolen sweaters. They held gray wool hats in their hands and parted as Lucas walked toward the altar.

Schulz introduced Father Bauder. Lucas approached the altar, crossed himself, turned, and raised both arms. The miners bowed. He recited his memorized prayer: "Lord God, cast your blessings on these brave men who risk their lives every day in this mine to provide livelihood for their families and all peoples of the Upper Donau. Amen."

The miners called out, *"Gluck auf,"* the customary greeting for wishing a fellow miner good luck on getting out of the mine alive.

Lucas kept his face prayerfully down to avoid eye contact with the miners. Maier and Schulz motioned to Lucas and walked toward their Hunde. Schulz said, "Thank you, Father. Come and we'll see you out."

Lucas stood still. "Please, I am overcome with this moment in this sacred place. If I may, I'd appreciate spending some time in prayer . . . alone in the chapel."

The two officials stepped aside amid whispers.

Maier said, "It would be against the rules and highly irregular to leave the priest alone in the mine."

"I suppose so," Schulz said as he set his jaw and squinted in thought. "But what harm could he do?"

Maier threw up his hands and nodded. Schulz returned to Lucas, smiled, and shrugged his shoulders. "Of course. Why not? Would one hour be enough time for you?"

"Yes. Thank you. I will pray for you and the miners."

4

The officials made their way out of the chapel. The miners opened a side closet and slipped into their jumpsuits.

Lucas walked to the picture of St. Barbara, bowed, and prayed he'd leave the mine alive. After five minutes he checked each side, saw no one, and stood, arms folded, in the center of the chapel.

After what seemed like an eternity, a miner stepped from the shadows and handed Lucas a headlamp and a folded piece of paper. He nodded in the opposite direction and whispered, "Take the next opening on the right."

Lucas nodded, put the paper in his pocket, slipped on his headlamp, and walked along a darkened tunnel. He squeezed through a small crevice and farther along saw a faint yellow light that created distorted shadows. After two steps he froze. White ghosts floating below with bobbing headlamps—men who would surely recognize him by day—passed within a meter of where he stood.

After they had gone by, Lucas looked over his shoulder, slipped into an unlit side tunnel, and walked some fifty meters.

His mind raced. I've never been so alone. Must focus, he told himself. Yet there was Erika on their special night, smiling at him by candle light, pillows askew, bedding tossed aside. *Stop this.*

The yellow spot of his headlamp danced along the rock-salt wall as he ran his hand over a daggerlike excrescence. He saw a rotting plank inscribed in faded red paint: *Eingang verboten* (keep out). He leaned forward and could see a square opening near a staircase, beyond which were two wooden slides covered with waxed oak with raised edges on either side. He thought he must be lost, but looked again at his map and saw the point labeled SLIDE. He shrugged, crossed himself, and prayed.

Again his mind flashed to a golden time with Erika at the Prater in Vienna and their small hotel in Grinzing.

He took a deep breath and stepped to the top of the slide. He sat down and grabbed the raised edges, his legs pointing down. He slid both feet across the slick oak, knowing that when he released the edge he would plummet into darkness. He crossed both arms across his chest, his hands trembling. His head was thrown back as he rocketed down the slide. His headlamp flashed along glistening purple and green salt rock. After the slide ended, he tumbled into a large room, losing his headlamp and shattering his glasses. He put the headlamp back on and tossed the glasses behind stacked lumber. He cocked his head and listened, hearing only the pounding of the hammer in his chest and his breathing, which sounded like an alpine gale. He drew his tongue over dry lips and felt as though an evil vise was clamping off his air. Then he heard a new sound: the metallic ping of water dripping somewhere in the darkness.

He thought of his father, Edouard, and was saddened that his father hadn't trusted him enough to personally inform him about the mission. Lucas regretted not telling his father that he loved him often enough. Yet a bigger regret was having never heard his father say those three words to him. He knew he wasn't to blame for his mother's death when he was born, but Edouard had blamed him for too many years. Lucas prayed for another chance with Edouard and with Erika, his soul mate.

Immersed in inky blackness one mile deep in the cold bowels of this labyrinthine salt mine, Lucas wiped sweat from his face with the salt-encrusted sleeve of his jumpsuit. The brine burned his eyes.

He pulled the scrap of paper from his pocket, directed his headlamp to the hand-drawn map, and with a trembling finger traced the inscribed route.

He ducked under an outcropping of black rock, and his shoe squeaked when he stepped onto a plank walkway for wheelbarrows. Lucas grimaced and caught his breath; he'd failed to change shoes. He paused and listened again—only dripping water, fainter now.

He walked through two empty chambers and focused his headlamp on his watch. It had been fifteen minutes since he left the chapel. His heart raced as he crept through a passageway into a cavernous space lined on all sides with scaffolding and shelves of raw lumber stacked with wooden crates—the Mineral Cabinet. He'd found it. He opened a small box and his headlamp illuminated hundreds of gold rings. Mixed with the rings were small irregular pea-sized gold nuggets. He picked up a handful and held them to his cheek. They were cold as death. He shuddered, realizing that he was holding gold human tooth fillings.

He stumbled on a four-by-four-foot object wrapped in white canvas and opened it. Lucas drew back, amazed at the brilliance of the gold necklace in Gustav Klimpt's *Lady in Gold.*

He stepped against a much larger crate. Protruding between

its planks was some kind of religious panel. He gasped. Casually strewn about on cardboard were panels of the *Ghent Altarpiece, The Adoration of the Mystic Lamb,* its resplendent color unblemished after more than five centuries. Overcome by his sense of art history of the Van Eyck polyptych from Joos-Vijd Chapel in St. Bavon Cathedral in Ghent, Belgium, he recognized a lower panel: *Soldiers of Christ.* His eyes were drawn to a knight in silver chain mail riding a white steed with braided mane. Across the chamber he saw a large wooden crate. He raced to it and pried open the lid. He wiped away covering straw and found a crate holding a bulky marble statue: the *Madonna of Bruges,* a large sculpture by Michelangelo of Mary cradling the infant Jesus.

Mission done; time to leave.

Lucas froze as cold steel jabbed into the back of his neck. He heard a pistol cock.

A derisive voice said, "Raise your hands, Brunn."

Lucas obeyed, turned, and stared into the Wehrmacht guard's face, shadowed by his coal-scuttle-shaped helmet. "Horst Schrader, is that you? What are you doing here? You don't belong with them. Only two years ago we were college classmates."

Schrader slammed the butt of his Luger pistol against Lucas's skull. Lucas dropped to his knees and rolled onto his back, fearing death. Schrader jumped astride his chest, his knees pinning Lucas's shoulders to the clay floor. Schrader spat in Lucas's face and slammed his fist into his nose. "I can't believe you're with these Resistance scum. How foolish. You will die for this." He grabbed Lucas by the neck and began choking him.

In a flash Lucas broke the chokehold, reached under his cape, grasped the knife, and plunged it into Schrader's chest—and left it there. A garnet geyser spewed from around the knife and splashed over Lucas's hands and face. The knife handle rocked back and forth with the slowing beating of the Nazi's heart. Schrader dropped like a stone, open eyes staring at eternity.

Lucas trembled. My God, what have I done? he thought, and felt for a pulse in Schrader's neck. Nothing. He dragged the limp body into a small side chamber and covered it with rock salt. Perhaps it would be several days before the man was discovered. Sweat pouring down his face, gasping for breath, Lucas adjusted his priest's clothing and headed toward the slide.

He ran through a small chamber littered with empty beer bottles and lumber stacked against the cragged walls. He flashed his headlamp around the room and saw a large crate standing against the opposite wall. He opened his small toolbox, grabbed a wire pliers, and cut the lock on the crate. It was empty except for scrap lumber, a dusty pack of condoms, and an odious, dead black rat.

Lucas backed away. Should he get Schrader's body and hide it in the crate? A wave of nausea swept over him. He gagged and vomited. No time. His left shoe came untied. Lucas leaned against the crate as he bent down to tie his shoe. The crated moved, just slightly. He reached behind the crate, slid it away from the wall, and saw an opening two meters in length and width. He shone his headlamp inside and saw a flat rock on the center floor, then squinted and saw the corner of a rectangular crate wrapped in white canvas. He removed the covering rocks and found a polished pine box, its top secured with eight cross-slotted flat-head screws. He knelt and looked closer. Inscribed on the top of the box was the letter *J*, and stamped on its side a stenciled image of the Eiffel Tower. His heart pumped faster. He opened his small toolbox, grasped a Phillips-head screwdriver, and removed the screws. Lucas lifted the lid and saw a rectangular object encased in a royal-purple velvet sleeve with a drawstring. Lifting the object from the fitted space and releasing the drawstring, he removed the rectangular frame and caught his breath. *J? La Joconde?* Could it be? Her enigmatic smile washed over his soul. Wherever he moved, her eyes followed, searing into his brain the realization that he was alone with the *Mona Lisa*. How many people in the world, other than da Vinci, had been blessed with such an audience? She smiled at him; he smiled back and drank in the beauty of her seductive brown eyes. Lucas leaned closer and saw the craquelure on her face, networks of small cracks and lines in the poplar wood panel on which she was painted. These horizontally arranged lines were born of da Vinci's genius and centuries of world adoration. With the index and middle fingers of his right hand he touched her face just below her left eye. Imagining the cracks as pores in her skin, he jerked his fingers away as though he'd committed a sacrilege. He closed his eyes and thanked God for this moment in his life.

He wanted to run. What was he doing in this place? But how could he leave her? He couldn't take her with him. His heart pounded, and his breaths came in gasps as he tried to think. He glanced at the wall and ten meters away saw another shadowed vertical crevice. He replaced the *Mona Lisa* in the purple pouch, secured the screws in the crate and wrapped it in the white canvas as he'd found her. He lifted the *Mona Lisa* and carried her like a babe in arms to the crevice. Reaching into the crack, he discovered a three-by-two-meter space filled with scrap lumber and jagged salt rock. He removed the lumber, slid the *Mona Lisa* into the space, scattered lumber over the crate, and covered it with black and green rock salt. He saw a small banana-shaped rock, picked it up and stood it on end, leaning against the right side of the crevice; his sentinel rock. He kicked dust over it so that it was hardly noticeable. Someday I will return here, he vowed to himself.

He walked from the chamber into the main tunnel and jogged for fifty meters. He stopped, leaned forward, hands on knees to catch his breath.

He found the stairway beyond the slide landing, ripped off his jumpsuit, and raced up two steps at a time to the main tunnel.

When he returned to the chapel, a janitor was sweeping the floor. He looked up in surprise and said, "Father, are you still here?"

Lucas gathered himself and tried to smile. "Oh yes, I'm afraid I got lost."

"Where is your jumpsuit?"

"I took it off and left it—I don't know where."

The janitor paused, removed his gray felt hat, and reverently held it in his hands. "That's all right, Father, we'll find it." He paused. "I don't want to step out of place, but may I ask a favor of you."

Lucas sighed. "Of course. What is your name?"

"Albert," the janitor said, studying his broom. "Would you please give me your blessing?"

"Of course."

Albert knelt and Lucas stepped to him and placed his right hand on the janitor's shoulder. "May God bless you, my son, Alton."

Wiping tears from his eyes, the janitor rose. "My name is Albert, but thank you, Father."

"I'm sorry."

"That is no problem." The janitor pointed. "The railway is straight ahead."

As Lucas walked toward the Hunde, Albert called out, "And Father, gluck auf."

Lucas rode his Hunde to the main entrance. The guard waved him through, and when he stepped outside, snow flurries were gusting into the mine entrance. He held his right forearm across his face. Sheets of ice covered the road, and as he looked for the guard shack, he slipped and fell. He got up, retched, and vomited into the snow.

The guard called and motioned. "Come in and wait here by the stove, Father." He shined his flashlight on Lucas's face. "You have puke on your cape and blood on your face. What happened?"

"Thank you, Ernst. I got nauseated on the road and fell."

The guard switched off the flashlight and helped him wipe his face clean. "Would you like a bowl of soup?"

Lucas stood, gathering his cape. "No, thank you. I must go now. I appreciate your kindness."

"I will call for help. They will take you to your hotel."

"No," shouted Lucas. "I have a ride coming. Don't call anyone." Lucas ran toward the main road.

The guard watched Lucas hurry away and reached for his telephone.

5

In the mine director's office, Schulz and Maier were having a beer and discussing the priest's visit. They sat in high-backed leather chairs facing a blazing fire in a stone fireplace.

"It amazed me," said Maier, "that you granted Father Bauder permission to remain in the chapel alone. That is not in accordance with visitor protocol."

"I know, but he seemed harmless enough, and I knew the janitor was due to clean the chapel. I'm sure he would notice any irregularities."

Schulz rubbed his chin and looked out of the window. "It's snowing."

"Don't change the subject. You could call the church in Bad Aussee and verify that this priest is indeed from there."

"Why are you so suspicious?"

"I just have a strange feeling about him. I can't explain it. I challenge you to call Bad Aussee."

"What time is it?"

Karl Maier stood. "It is time to make that call."

Schulz pressed a button on his desk, and his assistant promptly knocked twice and came into the room. "You rang, sir?"

"Felix, would you call the Catholic church in Bad Aussee? I'd like to speak to any of the priests who might be there."

"Right away, sir." Felix turned and left the room.

Schulz drank the last of his beer, set the decorative mug on a side table, smacked his lips, and sat back in his chair. "I think this is a waste of time, but I respect your feeling. So, we shall see . . . I hope."

A few minutes later, Felix returned. "No priests are there. The night security guard answered; he's on line one."

Schulz picked up his phone. "Good evening, this is Herr Heinrich Schulz, director of mines in Oberdonnau. To whom am I speaking?"

"I am Dirk Hartwig of church security."

"I was hoping to speak to a priest."

"I'm sorry, sir, but there are no priests in the church in the evening. Which priest do you wish to speak to?"

Schulz leaned forward. "I don't have a name. Perhaps you can answer my question."

The line was quiet for a moment. "I will try, sir."

"Good. Can you tell me if a new priest has arrived there recently? His name is Father Stefan Bauder."

"We have several priests, perhaps five or so. I don't recognize that name, but I don't know all of their names, mostly those who have been here for years. Sorry."

"Thank you, Dirk. You've been most helpful. Good-bye."

Schulz hung up and buzzed for Felix. He stood and met his assistant at the door. "Ask the janitor in the chapel to report to me immediately."

"Right away, sir, but I should tell you first that the guard at the entry outpost rang and asked to speak to you."

"Send a replacement and bring him here."

Maier rose from his chair. "Do I detect some doubt?"

"I'm beginning to wonder." Schulz lit another cigar.

"If indeed Bauder is a fraud and spy," Maier asked, "Saint Michael's here in Altaussee must be involved. How else could this have happened? Could the priest be sympathetic to the criminal Austrian Resistance?"

Schulz stared out the window; darkness hid the snow.

There was a knock, then Felix escorted the janitor into the room.

Schulz rose and shook the janitor's hand. "Thank you for coming. What is your name?"

"Albert, sir. Have I done something wrong?"

"No, not at all. I would like to ask you a few questions about the priest who blessed the miners in St. Barbara's Chapel this evening."

"Yes?" Albert looked around the room, his hands clasped in front of him.

"Did you meet the priest?"

"Yes, but he was not there when I first arrived for work."

"When did he come in?"

Albert rapidly blinked his eyes and rubbed his hands together. "I had almost finished cleaning the chapel, perhaps an hour or so after I started."

Schulz and Maier moved closer to Albert.

Maier asked, "Did you notice anything unusual about his behavior? Was he carrying anything, like a package or box?"

"Well, he seemed nervous. I asked him for a blessing and told him my name. After the blessing he forgot my name and seemed in a hurry to leave."

"Yes, go on. Anything else?"

"He said he got lost and was hot, so he took off his jumpsuit and left it somewhere."

"Was he wearing glasses?" Schulz inquired.

Albert stared at the ceiling, blinking his eyes. "I don't remember seeing glasses."

Schulz looked at Maier. "Anything else?"

The art restorer shook his head.

Schulz said, "Thank you, Albert. You may return to your work."

As Albert left, the assistant said, "The guard is here."

"Send him in."

Ernst came in and was seated in a straight chair in the center of the room.

Schulz inquired, "You asked to speak to me?"

Ernst, seemingly enjoying himself amid such powerful company, said, "Yes, I did, sir. I would like to report my concerns about the visiting priest."

"What are your concerns?"

Ernst shifted in the chair, leaning forward. "He seemed very young to be a priest, but then he said he was just appointed to his first parish in Bad Aussee. According to his papers, he is from St. Polten. He said he was familiar with Niedling as good farm country. Well, I'm from that area, and everyone knows that Niedling is mostly an area of dairies and cattle ranches, not many farms."

"What about his accent?" asked Maier.

Ernst thought a moment. "I didn't notice anything unusual."

Schulz started to speak, but Ernst interrupted. "I took his photograph."

Schulz jumped up. "Do you have the film?"

Ernst handed him the camera.

The director turned to Felix and passed him the camera. "Have the picture developed immediately."

"Yes, sir." Felix hurried from the room.

Schulz nodded to Ernst. "Go ahead with your story."

"Well, after the ceremony, when he came back, his face was covered with blood and he had vomited on his cape. I took him into the shack and tried to clean him up a little. I told him I would call for transportation to his hotel. His hands were shaking, and he spoke very fast. He said, 'I have a ride' and ran down the road." Ernst paused. "Is there some problem with the priest?"

"We don't know yet," said Schulz. "Thank you. You are relieved of duty. Your replacement will finish your shift for the night. Good work." He turned to Felix. "Call the Gestapo. Alert all local train and bus stations and the Salzburg Airport." Schulz rubbed his chin, pensive. "And include all airfields in Salzkammergut."

6

When Lucas reached the main road, he proceeded to the wooden gate to the motor vehicle repair yard. Fifty meters ahead automobile lights flashed twice, and he ran toward them.

Otto opened the right front door, and Lucas tumbled into the seat and pulled the door shut.

Otto stared at Lucas. "You're bleeding. What happened?"

Struggling to breathe, Lucas motioned for Otto to drive ahead. They rode in silence until they reached the road leading to the church cemetery.

As they approached, Otto slammed on the brake and pointed to a man wearing an overcoat and smoking a cigarette. He stood between two black sedans parked near the church entry.

They parked two hundred meters away behind a copse of trees with a sight line to the church.

"What happened in the mine?" Otto asked.

"It's classified."

An hour later four men in black trench coats came out of the church and drove away. After thirty minutes Lucas said, "I'll walk from here. Park the car and go to bed."

"But—"

"Do as I say." Lucas glared at Otto, got out, and limped toward the church. A dim light shone through a window next to the side door.

Lucas tapped the door three times.

Father Messmer snapped it open. "Thanks be to God, you have returned. Come in."

Lucas stepped inside and Father Messmer hugged him as though he was the prodigal son.

Breathing fast, the priest said, "The Gestapo was here and questioned me. Can you believe it? They said a thief stabbed a Wehrmacht guard in the mine. Did you—"

"Are you sure they said 'thief'?"

"Yes. And they even asked if I had left the church this evening." The priest bowed and fingered his rosary. "I am so afraid. They are searching every home and building in the village. We must pray."

"In time, Father. Did they say what was stolen?"

"They only mentioned a priceless work of art and asked if I knew anything about a visiting priest." Father Messmer bowed his head, slowly raised it, and dabbed his eyes with a white hand-kerchief. "They searched me. Such a sacrilege."

Lucas held his friend close. "Don't worry, Father."

"They ordered me to report to headquarters tomorrow morning." Gathering himself, the priest continued, "Now, go get cleaned up and change your clothes. Then you can tell us what happened."

A half hour later, Lucas returned wearing green lederhosen, long white socks, a shirt, and a gray vest. He described the events: the gate guard, meeting the mine officials, his prayer in St. Barba-ra's Chapel, finding *The Mystic Lamb*, and stabbing the guard. He made no mention of the *Mona Lisa*.

"Poor boy. Praise God that you were not injured." Father Messmer began to pace. "Then it's true. The trucks are hauling stolen art into the mine." He stopped and turned to Lucas. "Your father called. He is worried that you had not returned. He will be here soon." The priest removed a round silver watch on a chain from his gown, glanced at it, and frowned.

A quarter hour later, Edouard Brunn tapped on the door and came in. He hurried to Lucas and hugged him. "Are you all right, son?"

Lucas looked up sadly at his father. He was overcome with regret for disappointing him yet again, this time, perhaps the worst of all. He mumbled, "I'm sorry, Father. I tried . . . but I failed."

"Tell me what happened."

Lucas repeated the saga, adding a few details, but again not mentioning the *Mona Lisa*.

Standing a few inches taller than his son, Edouard had sandy, gray-streaked hair and broad shoulders. Above his square jaw, blue eyes reflected worry and years of sadness. He stepped back, forcing a half smile. "I have a surprise for you."

"What?"

"You will see."

A short time later, another knock sounded at the door, and Lucas's fiancée, Erika, stepped into the room. She pressed her hands to her cheeks and flew into his arms. She kissed him full on his mouth and stepped back, smiling. "Where have you been?"

Lucas stared at this lady who he hoped would someday be his wife. Her auburn tresses tumbled onto her shoulders and framed her face, which was the image of a Madonna. She wore a blue dirndl skirt accented with edelweiss, a white blouse, and red sweater. The irises in her brown eyes had tiny copperlike flakes that sparkled when she talked, and when she laughed, they flashed like shooting stars.

She had the trim body of an athlete: strong arms and tapered legs that had helped her score goals in soccer when playing against the boys. Her lips were full, soft, and kissable.

There was another knock. The priest opened the door, and Abel Graf limped in, leaning on a cane with his left hand.

Abel surveyed the group and smiled. "So, are we having a reunion?"

Lucas hugged his lifelong friend. "What's wrong with your leg?"

"It is good to see you, too." Abel smiled.

"I'm glad you're here. You know that."

The priest, Edouard, and Erika greeted him.

Dressed in tan lederhosen, a gray sweater, and a green hat, Abel stood two hands shorter than Lucas. He was dark skinned with thick hair the color of ebony that matched his mustache. His brown eyes narrowed as though expecting danger as he shook Father Messmer's hand. Lucas remembered his eyes widening with joy as he spoke in happier days. He hadn't seen him in two years, but learned through his family that he had signed onto a Liberian freighter as the wireless operator. He accidentally received secret messages from a Turkish drug cartel and immediately notified authorities at their next port of call. When they docked, he tried to escape but was arrested with the rest of the crew as inspecting officials unloaded a hidden cache of cocaine. Abel wound up in a Port Said jail for an unknown time, but mysteriously escaped. His whereabouts were unknown until he got a job in communications with a shipping company in Tirane, Albania. Lucas hadn't known if he was even alive until three weeks earlier when he received his letter with a date of return to Altaussee.

Abel had muscular arms and a pianist's hands with tapered fingers and trimmed nails.

Lucas thought back to his fingers gliding over the keys of his shortwave radio and stared at his nails. "Been on your radio often?"

"Some. I arrived two days ago for the Resistance Committee meeting. I voted with the other members that you were the man for this mission."

Erika interrupted. "Would someone please tell me what you are talking about?"

Lucas placed his fingers over her lips. "In a moment."

Father Messmer touched Lucas's shoulder. "Did you stab the Nazi guard?"

"Yes. He was Horst Schrader . . . he tried to kill me."

Abel, Erika, and the priest gasped.

Erika said, "I am not surprised that he joined the Wehrmacht. Horst was always a loser, even in high school, always trying to touch me."

"He hit me with his gun," Lucas said. "When I fell, he jumped astride my chest and pinned me down with his knees. He tried to choke me, but I broke his hold and stabbed him with the knife you gave me. It saved my life."

The priest gasped. "Is he dead?"

"I think so. He had no pulse in his neck."

Abel spoke in a demanding tone. "We must leave *now*."

Erika screamed, "No!"

Lucas led her into an adjoining room. "Erika, I love you with my heart and soul, but I can't stay here."

She thought for a moment and cupped her right hand on his cheek, fingers extended.

Lucas kissed her and touched the bracelet on her right wrist. He fondled the dangling gold heart. "You're still wearing it."

She put her hand over his. "Of course. I'll wear it always. You gave it to me on . . . our special night."

Lucas held her shoulders and looked into her eyes. "I don't know what to do. If I stay, the Nazis will arrest me, and you know what that means. There's a lot going on that you don't know. It's safer this way." He paused. "I will come back to you."

Her eyes filled with tears, and she took a deep breath, as though preparing to utter life-changing words. "I understand. I love and trust you and will be here when you come home."

As they returned to the main room, the priest pointed his cane at Abel. "If Lucas runs, they will hunt him down—and you with him." He turned to Lucas. "My son, if you run, you will never see Erika and your father again."

Erika squeezed Lucas's arm and looked at Father Messmer. "He's right, Father. He must go. I understand. He knows best."

Edouard hugged his son. "I agree, but first I must give you this." He handed Lucas a sealed tan envelope wrapped in clear plastic and bound with heavy cord.

"What is it?"

"Thousands of lives depend on the information in this envelope. You must not read it. Hide it in a secret place known only to you. Swear that you will do as I say."

Lucas nodded, hugged his father, and slipped the envelope into his lederhosen pocket.

Lucas held Erika at arm's length. "It's time." He moved toward the door.

She gasped and held her right hand over her heart.

"I am leaving." Abel limped from the room.

Father Messmer said, "Wait." He reached into his pocket, removed a gold amulet and chain, and slipped it around Lucas's neck. "This is for you, my son."

Lucas kissed Erika hard and raced through the door.

Father Messmer hugged Erika. "St. Christopher goes with him."

Lucas approached Abel standing by his motorcycle. "What's wrong with your leg?"

Abel threw his right leg over the seat, slipped his cane in the sidecar, and kick-started the Daimler-Puch motorcycle engine. "Get in."

Lucas climbed into the sidecar, and they roared into the night. They raced through the village along Kirchestrasse. As they came to the pathway leading to his mother's grave, Lucas slapped Abel's shoulder and shouted, "Stop."

Abel pulled to the side of the road, letting the engine idle. "We can't stay here."

"Two minutes," Lucas said. "I want to say a prayer with my mother."

Abel shook his head, switched off the engine, and pushed the bike behind a pile of rocks.

Lucas ran to the grave, bowed, and placed his hand on his mother's headstone. He read the inscription: "Gott Weiss Varum" (God Knows Why). After he prayed, he picked up a pointed spade his father kept at the graveside and dug a rectangular hole behind the headstone. He removed the envelope from his trousers. Should he read it? He'd sworn not to. He buried the envelope, patted down the sod, and placed a small square rock over it.

When Lucas returned, Abel stood by the bike. "So, are you ready to travel now?"

"What happened in Graz?"

Abel looked away and said nothing.

"The priest told me you were running from the Gestapo."

"The padre talks too much."

"And you don't share secrets with your brother?"

"Would you please get in?"

"Where are we going?"

"Somewhere the Nazis would never look for you."

"Don't tease me. Where?"

Abel said, "You remember flying for the businessman in Salzburg?"

Lucas nodded.

"Where is the airplane kept?"

"Obertraun, but what does that have to do—"

"We are going to fly to Graz."

"You're mad."

Abel threw up his hands. "It's our only hope. Remember: the Gestapo are after me as well as you."

Lucas nodded and looked up the road. "What if the plane's not there? And we have nowhere to hide?"

"Father Messmer arranged a safe place for us in Hallstatt."

"Where?"

"Im das Bonehaus."

"The Bone House? Are you crazy? How can we get in?"

"Father Messmer knows the priest there. He hid a key for us. I have the directions."

Lucas threw up his arms. "We can't travel along the main route. They'll have roadblocks at St. Agatha. And even if we could make it there, Hallstatt is such a small village. Someone will see us and call the Wehrmacht. I'm so afraid. Maybe we should go back."

"We are not going on the main road. I'll take L701. It's rough, but usually deserted at night."

"Then what? I don't want to sleep in a room with skulls. Where do we go tomorrow?"

"Obertraun. Don't worry, I'll take care of you."

"I know you'll try, but what can we do? There will be roadblocks. They'll be watching the trains and buses, and we certainly can't go on your motorcycle. There is no way to hike over Hoher Dachstein."

"I know," Abel said. "And they'll have the dogs on your scent, searching rivers, the forest—the entire countryside." He raised his arms and let them slap against his thighs.

"And you have an answer to all those problems."

"I have an apartment in Graz. You can hide there—as long as you need to."

"It's impossible."

Abel hugged Lucas and slapped him on the back. "Do you want to see your father and Erika again?"

Lucas climbed into the sidecar, and they started toward Hallstatt.

7

December 25, 1944

Brisk alpine winds swept across Altausseer See, stirring waves and flattening Edouard Brunn's trousers as he stood next to his wife's gravestone. Ever since her death, Edouard had gone there each morning before heading to his classroom. On Sundays he gathered bouquets of wild flowers and placed them at the base of her headstone. He found peace and clarity of mind standing close to her. But now there was no peace, and his mind was jammed with frightening possibilities. Would Lucas be caught and killed? Was he guilty of murder? Any murder would be unfathomable, but the murder of a Wehrmacht soldier while on a treasonous mission would be punishable by a painful execution. What if the Nazi soldier in the mine had died? Kaltenbrunner might be lying. Had they really photographed Lucas? If the guard had survived, he would name Lucas, and the Gestapo would soon arrest him. Where could he run and hide? There were no answers. Edouard decided to go to his classroom. The school was closed for the Christmas holiday, but perhaps he could find peace and solitude alone with his formulas.

He walked back to the road and drove to the Altaussee Gymnasium. His chemistry classroom had twenty desks with attached seats. One wall of windows opposite the door offered a spectacular view of the Loser, the landmark mountain of Altaussee. A Nazi flag hung in one corner, and on the wall opposite the windows were pictures of Adolf Hitler and August Eigruber, governor of Lower Donau. Edouard and all the teachers had received directives from Eigruber on the curriculum to be taught in all subjects and grade levels. The overriding directive emphasized the doctrine of anti-Semitism. It disgusted Edouard. How could such a draconian doctrine of genocide relate to chemistry, or indeed to mankind?

On the blackboard at the front of the room were various chemical formulas and equations. How he loved them. They were an integral part of his being. Each carbon, hydrogen, and oxygen radical was precious to him.

His mind flashed to his graduate studies at Karl-Franzens University in Graz and his doctoral thesis: "Relative Metal Bonding Capacities of Epoxy and Cyanoacrylate Glues in Aeronautics." How excited he had been defending it before his professors and a young Luftwaffe officer, Oberlieutenant Hermann Goering.

In later years, when the wings of Messerschmitt 110s began falling off, even the highly intellectual pig Goering didn't remember his presentation. Edouard had kept the formula and its derivation of the epoxies hidden in his attic for all these years, until he put it in a sealed envelope wrapped in clear plastic and tied with simple cord. He wondered where Lucas had hidden it. He turned from the board and stared at the Loser. How magnificent.

Three Gestapo agents wearing black leather coats burst into the room, Lugers drawn. The leader said, "Professor Brunn, you are under arrest for treasonous crimes against the Reich." One of the agents snapped on handcuffs.

Edouard was led to a gray panel truck and put in the rear. Two of the agents climbed in with him and the third one drove. Edouard sat on a narrow metal bench along one side of the compartment. He turned to try to release some of the pressure on his hands and arms.

The two guards sat on the opposite side, their pistols trained on Edouard.

"You are making a bad mistake," Edouard said.

The guards only stared without responding.

"Where are we going?'

The larger of the two agents got up and slapped Edouard across the face, snapping his head against the side panel. "No talk."

Edouard heard the sounds of the village as they slowed to a stop. The back doors swung open, and the agents pulled him from the truck. They were at Nazi headquarters.

Nazi Kurt Greiner met them at the door. "Take him to Herr Kaltenbrunner."

Kaltenbrunner was seated at his desk and didn't look up as Edouard was shoved into the office.

Edouard said, "This is a mistake. I resent the humiliation."

Kaltenbrunner yawned into his hand and looked up at Edouard. "So, Professor Brunn, you are angry because you were humiliated?" The Nazi scoffed, and suddenly burst into a tirade. "Where is your son?"

"I don't know."

"Do you know he is wanted for treason and attempted murder?"

Attempted? The word stabbed Edouard's soul. "That's preposterous. Lucas would never hurt another human being."

Kaltenbrunner smirked. "You see, we have an eye witness."

Edouard wrinkled his eyebrows.

"Oh yes, a most reliable one: the victim, Sergeant Horst Schrader. His strong German heart survived the murderous attempt."

Edouard's heart pounded and nausea racked his body.

"And we have other incriminating evidence. The guard photographed your son disguised as a priest, and our experts matched this photograph with his gymnasium class picture."

Kaltenbrunner bolted to his feet and hurried to Edouard. "Your cowardly son stabbed an unarmed Wehrmacht soldier and left him for dead. Indeed, he was in a coma for several days, but awoke and gave a detailed report, identifying your son as his assailant. A janitor heard his call for help and brought him out to safety. This same janitor identified pictures of your son as the peculiar priest who'd given a prayer ceremony in St. Barbara's Chapel."

Edouard took a sudden interest his shoes.

"One other thing, Brunn. Father Messmer was convicted of involvement in this crime and was arrested this morning. However, for now I will allow him to be under house arrest in the church, under constant guard. I thought that might be a comfort to you as you await execution."

"You arrested a priest? God will punish you."

Kaltenbrunner returned to his desk and waved to a guard. "Take him away."

The same guards dragged Edouard to the truck. Doors slammed and he was seated as before. Underway, bells tolled and villagers shouted Nazi slurs from the street. After a few minutes he heard the engine whine as they started to climb. Their speed slowed. Edouard feared that he would be shot on the roadside. An hour later, rain pelted the truck and they drove even slower. Rain? Fog? Edouard squinted and slammed his eyelids shut. Mountains. They rolled to a stop. A guard kicked the rear doors open and shoved Edouard into darkness. Hands tied behind, he fell facedown in mud and snow. Rolling on his side, he saw through clumps of mud the faint outline of mountains fronted by one-story cement-block buildings. Between two of them, flaming torches illuminated the opening of a huge cave and a large sign with black block letters on white boards: ebensee camp.

Loudspeakers atop Nazi trucks blared a summons to all villagers to gather at noon at Nazi headquarters, Hotel Seevilla. Those failing to attend would be arrested. Rumors of the murder in the mine had spread overnight, and the people murmured to each other about stories of a stolen treasure.

Erika stood with her parents, listening to speculation on what the Nazis were up to. She looked at her father and wished he wasn't so tall. It was not good to stand out in a crowd in 1944 Austria. She reached for his hand and smiled. "Such a way to spend Christmas Day." Ursula Teuber nudged her daughter and nodded for her to keep her eyes straight ahead. As Erika turned, a mischievous smile crossed her face like a child scolded at school.

A Nazi officer burst through the door and strutted to the front of the gathering crowd. The sun's reflection from the eagle on his black cap caused Erika to squint. His arms were too long for his short torso, and he reminded Erika of caricatures of Viennese raconteurs she'd seen in the Hotel Seevilla lobby. He wore wire-framed glasses over eyes too close together on his ferretlike face.

He flashed a menacing smile and began to pace, his arms locked behind his back. The people became deathly quiet. In a high-pitched whine, he said, *"Ich bin Oberlieutenant Kurt Greiner."*

He stopped pacing and folded his arms. "We of the Reich are saddened by very tragic news."

Three Nazi troop carriers roared into the square, and thirty Wehrmacht soldiers, rifles at the ready, encircled the crowd.

His face flushed, Greiner strutted faster. "Last night in the salt mine, one of our Wehrmacht guards was murdered by a thief who stole a priceless work of art." He glanced at the mirrorlike shine on his black boots and brushed an imaginary dust particle from the sleeve of his black coat. "We have tried to help you improve your lives and become responsible citizens of the Fatherland. And what do we get as gratitude for this benevolence?" He wheeled around, veins bulging in his neck. "Murder, treason, and theft." He waggled his right index finger at the sky. "You have been warned of the penalty for those foolish enough to resist our plan for the Thousand-Year Reich. You can't resist us, yet there are those among you who still think you can. No more warnings.

"We will exact the punishment today. However, we can suspend that punishment. If the murderer and thief steps forward and confesses, then the rest of you may return to your homes." He paused. "If not, we will execute two villagers now."

The crowd gasped and started to run, but were pushed back by the soldiers.

A seventeen-year-old lad with blond hair stepped forward. "I'm the one you're looking for. I killed the guard."

Greiner walked to him and sneered. "Ah, so we have a hero in our midst. And just how did you kill our guard?"

The lad stammered, "Uh, I shot him—between the eyes."

"Go back to your mother."

An elderly man leaning on a cane stepped forward. "If I had the chance I would kill you and your henchmen. I confess to killing your soldier and will die happy in my eighth decade knowing that many of us will live to one day see a free Austria."

"Go home, old man. I think I'll choose men the same age as our soldier." Greiner leaped into the crowd, grabbed two men approximately twenty years old, and dragged them to the front. Their wives and children screamed and reached for their loved ones, but the Wehrmacht guards restrained them.

Greiner nodded to two soldiers. "Take them to the wall. Hands tied behind. No blindfolds."

The soldiers tied the two victims' hands and led them to face the stone wall of the bell tower. A hush fell over the crowd. "Kneel," cried Greiner. The men knelt. Greiner walked behind them, drew his Luger, and shot each man in the back of the head. Their bodies tumbled to the side and were then loaded onto a Nazi truck.

Then, as though nothing had happened, he spat in the dirt and strutted among the people, stopping at random in front of men, staring into their eyes for a frightening eternity, and moving on.

He paused before Erika and raised an eyebrow. He looked her up and down and smiled, a derisive smirk showing rotten teeth. He stood on his toes and looked up at Klaus. "Name?"

Erika's father snapped to attention and, in a military voice, said, "Teuber, Klaus, sir."

Greiner turned to Erika. "And your name, fraulein?" She gave her name, and he pulled a notepad from his jacket and jotted a note. "Do you have a boyfriend?"

Erika looked at her parents. They nodded. She said, "He is my fiancé, Lucas Brunn."

Greiner added a note.

He did a quick about-face and resumed his diatribe, gesticulating as he talked. "But we are honorable men and want to give you every chance. So we have decided to offer you an opportunity." Quiet descended on the villagers like velvet thunder. "Tell us who the foolish traitor is. He doesn't belong with you people, true patriots of the Reich."

He walked back to the front of the people, clasped his hands behind, and rocked up and down on the heels and toes of his boots. His voice again reeked with derision. "You will be handsomely rewarded." He turned, stepped toward the hotel, and snapped to a stop. The crowd waited. "I will be in my office in the hotel. Dismissed." His right arm shot out. "Heil Hitler."

Stunned, seemingly frozen in time, people moved to console the wives and children of the innocent victims. They looked at one another—family, friends, neighbors, as had been their ancestors. Slowly they began to disperse.

Erika caught up to her father. "What did he mean, Papi?"

Klaus's jaw muscles rippled and his lips were drawn into a fine line. He looked at his daughter without speaking.

His wife, Ursula, put her finger over pursed lips. "Shh." She put her arms around Erika, and they started for home.

———

Oberlieutenant Greiner strode into the hotel lobby, his boots clicking on the honey-colored wooden floor. He entered the main salon, where a long oak table and chairs dominated the oak-paneled room festooned with black swastikas and red-and-black Nazi flags. A picture of der Führer hung over the stone fireplace where a portrait of Johannes Brahms had hung for almost a century.

Greiner stepped up to the officer seated at the head of the table, snapped his heels, and shot out his right arm. "Heil Hitler."

The officer didn't look up, and Greiner remained at rigid attention.

Finally the commanding officer closed a folder and turned to Greiner. "So? Relax, Kurt."

Greiner said, "Your message has been delivered, my Obergruppenführer. I think we—you—gave the peasants something to think about."

Kaltenbrunner, a giant of a man towering more than six feet with massive shoulders and hands as wide as boat oars, had an enormous scar on his left cheek that stretched from his mouth to his left ear. He looked at the four officers seated at the table, waved to dismiss them, and nodded for Greiner to follow him to his private office.

They entered the office, and Kaltenbrunner motioned for Greiner to sit. He opened an engraved silver humidor embossed with a black swastika and offered Greiner a cigar, which he graciously accepted. "You have done well, Kurt. I've been keeping an eye on you."

The lieutenant sat up straight, bit off the tip of the cigar, and spat it into a spittoon. "I am at your service, sir."

"Do you think anyone will cooperate with us?"

Greiner lit his cigar and blew a stream of smoke away from his master. "You never know. It depends on their level of fear—and guilt."

Kaltenbrunner leaned forward, elbows on his desk. "And what of the other aspect of your surveillance?"

Greiner checked the door.

"Speak, man. No one listens at my door."

Greiner crossed his legs and smiled. "Well, I did notice one girl, perhaps eighteen." He shrugged. "She did have brown eyes, but a good body. *Bauern Fraulein*, farm girl, she has—" He opened his hands and spread his fingers like melons in front of his chest. "I think that the Obergruppenführer might find her most satisfactory."

"Name?"

"Erika Teuber. Klaus is the father. And she has a fiancé, Lucas Brunn.

"You cannot be serious. I just arrested his father. Interesting." Kaltenbrunner rubbed his chin and smiled. "Why don't we have Herr Teuber in for questioning?" As he thought, a feral smile distorted his scar. "And, Kurt, bring the entire family. Also, investigate this Brunn family." He smiled. "We may have found our murderer."

The Teubers returned home, having said nothing on their way. They sat in the living room, staring at each other.

Erika looked at her father. "Papi, what is the Resistance?"

Klaus said, "The Resistance is a group of men and women who hold our Austrian ideals and heritage dear. They don't like what the Nazis are doing to our homeland, taking our freedom from us. It all started with the Anschluss in 1938, when Hitler annexed Austria as part of Germany."

"Well, how can they do that, forbid people from living in freedom, as they wish?"

Klaus pulled his chair close to his daughter. "The Nazis force their will on people, on entire countries, by using a conspiracy of fear. If people don't comply with their wishes, they are disposed of, sent to concentration camps to do slave labor helping the Third Reich's war efforts—or worse, they are murdered."

Ursula said, "Klaus, she can't understand such things. I certainly don't. Let's not talk about it."

Klaus stood and kissed his wife. "My dear Ursula and Erika, we have to talk about it, because we have a personal problem with the Nazis."

Erika looked at her parents. "What could be worse than what they did today?"

"They can destroy our family," Klaus said. "Do you remember when you were a little girl when your mother died? Do you remember her?"

"Yes, her name was Grete, and she had beautiful eyes." She paused. "They were brown, I think. But what does that matter? There was sadness for years, but then you married Ursula, and she brought happiness back to our home."

"That is true, my Erika." Klaus paused and looked at Ursula, who nodded for him to proceed. "I must tell you something that is most difficult—and dangerous."

Erika started to speak, but Klaus put his hand over her lips. "Just listen, please. Your mother's father, your grandfather, was a rabbi in Poland. Your mother's eyes were indeed brown, as are yours." He held Erika's shoulders and their eyes locked. "Erika, you have Jewish blood in your veins."

Erika stood tall. "Yes, and I am proud of it."

"Never tell anyone what I've told you, not even Lucas. The Nazis would arrest you."

Klaus nodded and winked at his wife. "There is more. I met Ursula at the Volksoper in Vienna, and I fell in love with her. Before she agreed to marry me, she told me of a serious fact that could destroy our family as well. Ursula's maiden name was Czernin; she is of Jewish descent. Her first husband, Herr Lanner, aware of the changing political climate in Austria, had her papers expertly changed. I had your birth certificate changed as well."

"Wonderful," Erika said. "Then we have nothing to worry about."

Klaus wrapped his arms around his daughter and wife. "Come, let us light our fourth Advent candle." They sat before their Advent wreath made of straw covered with holly encircling four red candles.

Klauss nodded to Erika. "You have the honor of lighting all of the candles."

Erika scratched a match and lit each of the four candles. "Papa, may I say our prayer?"

Klaus looked at Ursula and nodded.

They held hands and bowed. Erika spoke in a soft voice. "Our heavenly father, be with us in these troubled times. Bless and protect our family. Dear God, give us hope. Amen."

3

Erika hurried into the bakery and slipped on her white apron. "Good morning Mr. Sonntag."

"Ah, Erika, late again. I would appreciate—"

"Sorry, I am not myself today." She threw her hands up. "I am so sad about what happened in the square yesterday. Those poor men were my friends."

"We will not speak of that here. Do you understand?"

Erika nodded and busied herself putting freshly baked loaves onto shelves. She remembered with disgust and hatred the Nazi officer and his rotten teeth. Why did he make a note after talking to her? She'd heard rumors that the chief Nazi officer was interested in young Austrian women.

The doorbell jangled, and Nazi officer Greiner entered, followed by Ernst Kaltenbrunner, who stooped to clear the doorframe.

Kaltenbrunner stood more than six feet tall and exuded confidence dressed resplendently in his Nazi officer's uniform, decorated with rows of bars and medals on his tunic. His acne-pocked face had an accusing frown, further distorting a massive scar from a fencing match during his law college days at the University of Graz.

Erika gasped, her hands trembled, and she dropped a loaf.

She knelt to pick it up, but Kaltenbrunner grabbed the loaf first, took Erika's apron, and wiped it off. "There, Fraulein, good as new." His eyes bored into her chest.

Erika blushed and put the loaf on a side shelf.

Kaltenbrunner slowly licked his lips, still staring at her breasts. "I'd like to buy a loaf of bread."

Herr Sontag stepped forward. "Please take as many of our fine loaves as you wish, our gift to you for the honor of having you in our little bakery. Did you notice our swastika outside?"

Kaltenbrunner reached for the loaf that Erika had dropped. "This one will be fine." He scattered coins on the counter and walked out, Greiner trotting at his heels.

Herr Sontag turned to Erika. "You should treat him with respect. Be nice to him. Smile. He decides if we live or die."

Frau Stossen came in with her basket for her daily purchase of bread. Usually forthcoming and friendly, she paid for her bread without speaking. She smiled at Herr Sontag, but only glanced at Erika, shook her head, and hurried out.

Erika threw her apron on the counter and dashed out of the bakery with Herr Sonntag ordering her to stay. She arrived at home, crying and wringing her hands.

Ursula ran to her. "What is wrong?"

Erika buried her head on her mother's shoulder. "Mother, I am so afraid."

"And what are you afraid of, child?"

"Have you heard the rumors that Herr Kaltenbrunner is romantically interested in young Austrian girls?"

"Who says that? I never heard such foolishness."

"All my friends are talking about it and won't speak to me. They think he is interested in me."

Ursula said, "Have you told Papa?"

"I couldn't bear it."

There was a loud knock at the door, and Frau Stossen barged into the room. "Ursula, you must leave at once."

Erika stared at her mother. "Mother?"

Ursula said, "What? I have done nothing wrong. Erika, you must go home with Frau Stossen. I'll wait here for your father. He will straighten this out."

Two black Mercedes sedans screeched to a halt outside.

Frau Stossen ran into the kitchen and out of the back door.

Erika shouted, "I must find Papa."

Kurt Greiner stormed into the house and grabbed Ursula. "You are under arrest for crimes against the Reich."

Erika reached for her mother, but Greiner pushed her back and she fell to her knees. A Gestapo agent picked Erika up, spun her around, and snapped on handcuffs.

"What are you doing, you swine?"

The agent slapped her across the face. Ursula screamed and leaned toward her daughter. Greiner cuffed Ursula and the Nazis dragged both women outside.

Greiner opened the back door of the leading Mercedes and pushed Ursula in. He pointed at Erika. "Put that one in the other car."

They drove fast to Nazi headquarters where Erika and Ursula were taken into the private office of Obergruppenführer Ernst Kaltenbrunner.

Kaltenbrunner said to Greiner, "Take the mother to the holding cell."

Erika cried, "No. I want to stay with her."

Kaltenbrunner nodded, and the soldier led Ursula screaming from the room.

Kaltenbrunner said to the guard, "Take off the cuffs and leave me."

Erika rubbed her aching wrists, glared at Kaltenbrunner, and started to speak.

The Nazi monster slapped her hard across the face. "No more talking. You and your mother are in grave danger."

Erika said, "Why? We have done nothing wrong."

"You are both are guilty of the worst of all crimes against the Reich. You are Jews."

Erika pleaded, "We are not. Our papers are in perfect order."

"Your papers are forged. Expertly forged to be sure, but they are your death sentences."

Erika wept, tears streaming down her face. "Please."

"I'm afraid there is nothing I can do. You are Jewish women posing as citizens of the Reich. That is a crime punishable by summary execution. You will both face the firing squad in the morning in the village square, with all the people watching."

Erika collapsed onto the floor.

Kaltenbrunner walked slowly around her, stalking his prey.

"Perhaps there is one way to spare both of your lives." He pulled Erika to her feet, softly brushed her hair from her face, and kissed her on the lips.

She spat in his face.

Kaltenbrunner punched her in the abdomen, and she dropped to her knees.

The Nazi removed a white linen handkerchief from his tunic, amd wiped his face. "As you wish. Then you both die tomorrow."

He led Erika to a leather chair next to his desk. "I will repeat my proposition. You move into Villa Kerry and live with me, sleep in my bed, and do as I say. No exceptions. If you do that, both you and your mother live. If you refuse, I'll have you tonight and send you to the wall with her in the morning. Your choice. You know, I like fire in my women. Answer me this minute." He slapped his hands on his hips. "Well?'

Erika stared at the floor and whispered, "All right." She trembled and sobbed. "My God, what will my parents think?"

"Tell me, what will your fiancé think?"

"How do you know about him?"

"Simple. You told my lieutenant his name in the square. Don't you remember?"

"Keep him out of this. He knows nothing of this."

Kaltenbrunner came close and lifted her chin. "Where is he?"

"I don't know."

"When did you last seem him?"

"A day or so ago."

"He is guilty of attempted murder. Has he told you about that?"

Erika studied her shoes.

"Have you been to bed with him?"

"That's none of your business."

"We shall see. Well, if you accept my proposition, at least your parents will be alive—and so will you. Of course, you will be forbidden any contact with this Lucas Brunn. We will make appropriate arrangements, and, Erika, you may even come to enjoy our relationship. I can show you things you have never imagined."

Erika spoke to the scar. "What will your wife think of this?"

He slapped her again, knocking her off balance. "You are never to speak of that again."

She glared at him and rubbed her cheek. "I have one condition."

Kaltenbrunner scoffed. "There will be no conditions."

"My parents must never know. It would kill them."

The Nazi stared at her and shrugged. "Fine. I will announce that you are now my official secretary and personal assistant." He yelled, "Greiner, release Frau Teuber."

Greiner went to the holding cell and unlocked Ursula's handcuffs. "You are free to go."

Ursula rubbed her wrists. "Where's my daughter?"

"She will remain here. She is quite safe."

"But why—"

Greiner grabbed her arm and escorted Ursula out of the hotel. A crowd had gathered. She ran into the waiting arms of Klaus. They embraced and started walking home.

Ursula said, "What do you think he meant by 'she is quite safe'?"

"I don't know, but I'm worried. The Nazis don't grant favors without asking for something big in return."

Ursula stopped and looked up into her husband's eyes. "You know what my worst fear is?"

"Yes, I do, but whatever it is, if Erika and you are safe, we have to count our blessings and get on with our life. It drives me crazy that I am powerless to intervene." Klaus kissed her and looked at the red marks on her wrists. "I'm glad you got rid of those bracelets."

10

Route L701 proved as quiet as Abel had guessed. They met few cars. Lucas listened to the low, steady hum of the Daimler-Puch engine as they climbed into heavy forest. Above the gray stone massif of Mount Dachstein, a gibbous moon shone like a pearl pasted onto a blue sky. The moon illuminated alabaster clouds floating above sparkling necklaces of pristine snow clinging to the cragged Alps.

The road widened and they arrived at Halstatter See. They stopped just outside of the village and parked the motorcycle behind a copse of pines. They hiked into the dark village and walked on opposite sides of the only street. Hallstatt was situated on a narrow shelf of land between the base of the mountain and Halstatter See. The shops were closed, house windows shuttered, and the village square deserted with no Christmas decorations.

They approached the cemetery next to the church and climbed up a steep grade of steps to the two-storied St. Michael's Chapel. A soft yellow light glowed through a gothic window on the ground floor. Abel paced four steps to the left of the Bone House door and moved a stone the size of an apple. He dangled a key chain and smiled at Lucas. They entered the first floor of the ossuary lined on three sides by shelves stacked with human skulls. At one end of the altar stood a large wooden crucifix with a sizable green stone at its base. The skulls were arranged in perfect rows and decorated with ornate floral crowns as well as inscriptions with family names, some with the date of death. Many skulls also lay scattered below the shelves.

Lucas said, "I've forgotten the story of the skulls."

"In the eighteenth century, they ran out of room for graves in the village, and the church would not allow cremation."

"They look like ivory."

Abel smiled. "Several years after a person's death, the grave was opened and the skull removed. It was left exposed to the sun and moonlight until it was ivory white. There are about twelve hundred skulls here, and roughly half are painted by hand and placed next to other family members. The ones with candles on either side were priests."

"What's this picture embedded in the floor?"

"It's the painter Michael's *Scales of the Soul*, placed there in the 1700s."

Lucas raised his eyebrows and walked to the window. He stood motionless, hands in pockets, staring at the headstones in the small cemetery.

Abel said, "What are you thinking about?"

Without turning, Lucas shook his head and remained silent.

"Worrying about them won't change the situation. Perhaps there will be some news when we arrive in Graz." He patted Lucas's shoulder. "When we get to Obertraun, act as though this is just a regular flight."

"Flight? What flight? This is crazy. I've flown business flights for Herr Kogel, but he always schedules them. I don't even know if the plane's there. What if it hasn't been serviced? What if they won't let me use the plane without his permission?"

Abel stared at Lucas. "Then we take it." He removed a folded map from his pocket and spread it on the stone floor. "Let's get to work on our flight plan."

Lucas knelt next to the map. "I've flown there many times."

"We're not going to Graz."

"What?"

"Let me explain. We're going to Gratwein—"

"I know it. It's on the route to Graz."

"Good. There's a dirt runway near a dairy farm on the River Mur, twenty kilometers from Graz. Father Messmer has arranged for a Resistance cell to meet us."

"I still have my doubts."

Abel flashed a flashlight across the sea of skulls. Ornate crosses, black shields, and flowers decorated the countless skulls inscribed with family names.

Lucas said, "What's upstairs?"

"I do not know. Maybe more bones."

"I'll sleep up there. Anything is better than this."

"No. We must stay on the ground floor. It's more secure. We could have unexpected company. Let's make plans for tomorrow."

Lucas sat down beside him, studying the map.

Abel drew a circle on the map. "We are here at Hallstatt." Then he drew an arrow and tapped his finger on the spot. "Here is Obertraun." He studied Lucas's face. "Now do you understand why we came here?"

"I don't think I like what you're thinking," Lucas said, shaking his head.

"Is this not where Herr Kogel keeps his airplane?"

"Yes, but—"

"It's our only chance. You can fly this airplane to safety."

"But this is illegal."

Abel shrugged. "Afraid you'll be arrested? You have no choice. Listen to me. It's 375 kilometers to Gratwein. Just north of the village is a dairy farm by the side of the runway. Do you remember it now?"

Lucas said, "It's probably not easy to land there, even in good weather."

Abel looked back at the map and pointed. "This is Mount Dachstein, three thousand meters high. We will have to gain altitude immediately after takeoff." He then drew a line to another point. "This is Pleschkogel, only one thousand meters. We should be able to go over it and fly straight in."

"I haven't flown in a year," Lucas said.

"I don't know. Maybe the plane has not been serviced."

"Don't make jokes."

Abel patted Lucas's shoulder. "I'm trying to get my pilot to relax."

"Can you use your radio in flight?"

Abel laughed. "And who would I call? The Luftwaffe?"

"Maybe you could call and find out about Father and Erika."

Abel grabbed Lucas by the jaw and looked into his eyes. "Don't think of them. Not now. If you ever want to see them again, you must concentrate on this flight plan."

"I understand. We'll probably have some rain, snow, and fog in the morning. Phyrnpass and Schoeber Pass will be a threat; high winds could blow us onto the rocks. We must also stay as low as possible to avoid radar."

Lucas held out his hands, palms up. "Do you really think the Luftwaffe will be searching for an ex-college student?"

"You, my friend, are no longer a student. To them you're a murderer and traitor." Their eyes locked. "To me you're a patriot." He paused. "Go to sleep."

11

Awakened by the din of a predawn storm, Lucas blinked and looked out the window. Lightning flashed, thunder rumbled, and raindrops pelted the gothic window. Last night's events flashed through his mind, and the dread returned. What were his chances of ever seeing his father and Erika again?

He shook Abel's shoulder.

Abel's eyes snapped open as he jerked his Luger from under his coat and aimed between Lucas's eyes.

Lucas raised his hands in mock surrender. "It's raining."

Abel put the gun away. "I hear it; the runway will be muddy. What kind of plane is it?"

"It's a biwinged Fiat." Lucas shook his head. "The final approach to Gratwein will be difficult in this weather. We must clear Pleschkogel, three thousand meters, and land from the northwest."

"How long have you been flying for Herr Kogel?"

"About two years. He has business in Graz, Salzburg, and Munich. Sometimes we haul small arms and ammunition. He's on the edge of the law, and I think sometimes crosses it."

"Why does he keep the plane in Obertraun?"

"His brother owns the airstrip."

"Do you know him well?"

"Not well. He's not a pilot. Just follows his brother's orders."

"I hope he has not been alerted about us. Go over the flight plan again."

"Compass heading to Gratwein, one four seven. With high winds the segment through Phyrnpass will be more dangerous. The last peak to clear is Pleschkogel, three thousand meters, so I'll have to climb higher than I'd like because of radar."

"I am trusting you with my life. You will do it."

Their eyes locked, and Lucas said, "We . . . will do it."

Abel put both hands on Lucas's shoulders. "You are a patriot. Come, it is time."

They put on their coats and left the Bone House at five-minute intervals. Walking on opposite sides of the street, they avoided eye contact with the few people they met. When Lucas got to the bike, Abel had removed the tarp and wiped down the seats.

Wet tree branches slapped them as they bumped along the rutted forest trail. They reached the main road and drove past the turnoff to Hallstatt. After two miles they came to a farm road crossing where a tractor blocked the highway. The owner was working on the engine and turned with a start at the motorcycle noise. Wearing a black rain slicker and boots, the farmer shouted, *"Gruss Gott."* Go with God.

Abel shouted back, "Gruss Gott. Would you please move your tractor so we can pass?"

"Engine dead—won't start."

Abel checked both sides of the road. There was no room to pass.

The farmer stared at Lucas. "Are you men from here?"

Lucas looked away, and Abel dismounted the motorcycle and walked to the tractor.

Lucas's heart raced as he watched his friend try to help the farmer with his dead tractor, a delay that could cost him his life. Soon the tractor's engine roared to life.

Abel returned and got back on the motorcycle. "There was nothing wrong with the tractor. I don't like this."

The farmer cleared the road and waved appreciation as they sped by. Lucas looked back over his shoulder as the farmer removed a radio with antenna from his pocket and held it to his ear.

Lucas said, "He's calling the Nazis. We can't go to Obertraun."

"There's no other choice."

They turned in the direction of Obertraun and met only one other farmer. His wife, a large woman with beet-red cheeks sat clutching a brown purse on the tractor fender. They waved.

Two kilometers before they reached Obertraun, Lucas slapped Abel's shoulder and pointed to a small gray building and a flapping, dirty, orange wind sock. They slowed and turned through a gate onto the airstrip encircled by a wire fence. On the apron two planes were tied down, protected by sheets of canvas supported by four poles at the corners. The rain had stopped.

Lucas walked to the gray building's door and pounded. Abel stood behind. Two more knocks. No response. Lucas glanced at Abel who threw both hands up and ran to the door.

Lucas said, "We should leave."

Abel took a step back and butted his shoulder into the door, knocking it off its hinges. He drew his Luger, and they leaped into the room. No one was there. Newspapers, beer bottles, and a plate of sausage were strewn haphazardly on a metal table with two wooden chairs. Abel walked to the telephone and ripped it from the wall, its black wires dangling.

Abel nodded toward the door of another room. Lucas threw open the door and Abel walked in, his gun drawn.

Cowering in a corner with his arms shielding his face, which was covered with black stubble, the man spoke to Lucas. "Please do not shoot me."

"We're not going to harm you, Karl. We want the Fiat."

Karl stood and raised his hands. He wore a black woolen jacket with deep pockets over a gray down nightshirt.

Abel said, "If you reach for your pocket, I will shoot you in the face."

Karl raised his trembling hands higher.

"Just give us the Fiat keys and we'll leave you."

Karl nodded and, with hands raised, walked into the office. He sorted through a ring of keys, selected two and handed them to Lucas. "This one is to the storeroom. There is no fuel in the Fiat."

Lucas stepped toward the door. "Let's go."

Abel walked to Karl and slammed his fist into his jaw. Karl sank to all fours. Abel grabbed his Luger by the barrel and crushed it into Karl's temple. He fell, motionless on the floor.

Lucas cried, "You shouldn't have done that. Will he wake up?"

"Probably."

"Should we tie him up?"

"No time. I'll refuel while you do the preflight check."

"You have to check out the wireless."

Abel waved okay, ran to the bike, retrieved a leather pouch, and entered a storage shed behind the office.

Lucas pulled off the canvas cover and looked at the biplane Fiat with its call number, K7437, stenciled in black on the mustard-yellow fuselage and its green and brown camouflage stripes. A World War I relic, the plane had been used as a fighter early in World War II, but it couldn't compete with the RAF's Spitfires and Mosquitoes. It remained an efficient craft with a range of seven hundred kilometers and speed of two hundred kilometers per hour. During his training, Lucas had come to feel confident flying it.

Lucas yanked the canvas cover off the engine, and a flash of lightning blinded him momentarily. He jumped onto the wing, slipped, and grabbed a wing strut to avoid falling. He removed canvas covers from the windshields and seats and climbed into the rear seat. He picked up a leather pouch, opened it, and put on a flyer's helmet and goggles. Lucas checked the wind sock; it was flapping straight out from stiff northeasterly winds.

Abel ran from the storage room carrying three large gasoline cans. After filling the gas tank he walked to the front of the aircraft and waved to Lucas to power up. When Lucas gave a thumbs-up, Abel cranked the propeller. The engine stuttered and belched black smoke. On the third try, the engine coughed to life. Abel climbed onto the wing, got into the front seat, and switched on the wireless. It squawked, and he immediately turned it off.

Lucas fired the engine and stepped lightly on the left rudder pedal. He nudged the throttle forward, and they taxied over the tarmac onto the muddy runway. The wheels buried into axle-deep mud. They started slowly down the runway, facing upwind. Rain blew in horizontal sheets. As he shoved the triangular-shaped control stick forward, he saw two green-camouflaged trucks crash through the wire fence.

He reached forward, slapped Abel's shoulder, and pointed at

the trucks. Puffs of white smoke came from the soldiers' rifles in the back of the truck.

Lucas slammed the control stick forward. Their wheels sank deeper into the mud. The trucks raced closer, trying to cut them off, maybe ram them.

Lucas went full throttle, and they lifted a few feet and gained speed. One of the trucks had a good angle to ram them. Abel fired his Luger at the driver. As their paths converged, the plane rose higher and bounced again. They lifted some ten meters from the runway's end as the truck zoomed under them, puffs of smoke coming from the rifles. Lucas ducked below the bulkhead as bullets tore into the left wing and shattered Abel's windshield.

Abel screamed, and Lucas felt the plane's nose lift almost vertically. Suddenly the engine stalled, and they hung suspended in air. The plane rolled and went into a spinning dive. Lucas yanked back on the stick with all his might. They leveled off and vanished into the fog.

Lucas strained to see Abel. Face bloodied, goggles smashed, Abel sat slumped forward on the instrument panel.

Lucas set his course, and in a half hour, the fog lifted a bit and he could make out the lake at Altaussee, next to the Loser Mountain. He must avoid that.

A sudden wind shear stacked the plane on its side. No control. White blindness. Climbing or diving? They broke through the clouds, and as the plane plummeted, he saw the earth spinning up at him. He immediately pulled back harder on the stick; still no control. The wind screamed and the plane shuddered. His mouth was dry as cotton, and his mind raced. Erika? Father? He pulled harder and felt some progress as the plane nosed up fifteen degrees. The engine noise split his ears; the wind buffeted his face. As the nose raised a bit more, the altimeter spun crazily, passing one thousand meters. Suddenly, they nosed down again, and lake's water rushed up at him. With a superhuman effort, he pulled back on the stick, and the nose lifted once more. He leveled off some one hundred meters above the water.

Lucas breathed for the first time in what seemed a lifetime. He wiped his goggles and peered straight ahead. Gray sky, water, and stone. Stone? He was speeding straight into the Loser. He jerked the stick back and slammed his foot onto the right rudder pedal. He felt a bone-shattering jolt as the plane's undercarriage slammed into an outcropping of rock. The plane spun in air.

His pilot instincts took over. Left wheel gone, propeller intact, altitude steady at five hundred meters. He craned his neck trying to see Abel. The collision had knocked him down farther into the seat, but Lucas could discern no movement. Panic shot through him, but he forced himself to stay calm. He looked down at the islands of fog floating beneath his wings. He could make out a village, his village, where tiny specks of people were running in the streets, looking up at him. The thought of his father in a con-centration camp blew a hole in his soul. Erika? He shut his eyes.

Okay, he coached himself, time for a situational analysis: copilot injured, possibly dead; aircraft disabled, left landing gear gone. Survival options: land immediately and care for Abel— negative, they'd be arrested and shot. There was only one choice. He must try to reach Gratwein where there would be help avail-able. Decision: Gratwein, and pray for a miracle.

He climbed to two thousand meters and set the compass heading. He cut the engine RPMs and maintained air speed at 175 knots. He nosed the plane toward a blue tunnel in the sky in the direction of Toplitz, the first checkpoint en route to Gratwein.

After ten minutes he saw peaks to his left and looked at his map. The tallest peak, Warscheneck, was 2389 meters. He corrected twelve degrees and flew into Phyrnpass. He was startled by an engine miss, but thankfully there was no repeat. Steady now, he told himself.

One hour later he saw another peak. He studied the map. Zeirtzkamper, 2126 meters. He corrected fifteen degrees to the right. While he completed the course correction, wind shear knocked the plane on its side. He strained against his seat harness, and the mountains turned upside down. His hand was knocked from the control stick when another blast righted the plane. As he flew into a cloud of white blindness, a shroud of mist encompassed him. The control stick bounded from one knee to the other. Lucas dropped his head and prayed hopelessly. He thought of Erika's smile and her bracelet.

He rubbed his gloved hand over the altimeter: four thousand meters. He was clear of the highest peaks. He thought of Luftwaffe radar and scanned the sky. It looked clear. He needed to be calm and think. He moved the stick and trimmed the plane to an acceptable vibration. Cloud density decreased. He looked down and saw a town: St. Michael. He was heading directly into Pleschkogel, three thousand meters. He smiled. He could make it.

As he cleared the peak, he saw the gray ribbon of the River Mur. The ceiling was five hundred meters as he dropped lower into his final leg. There, beyond the river, skimming the mountain tops, two F110 Messerschmitts approached in formation. He hugged the treetops and thought of vultures. He spotted a village—Gratwein. There, north of the village, he could make out a green field, brown and white cows, and a long white building. Across a fence, an orange wind sock blew horizontally toward the dirt runway.

Treetops near the river waved violently, the wind from the east. He would have to allow for drift and land on his first pass.

The vultures, black crosses on their wings, banked right and dove straight at him. He nosed the plane toward the runway. The wind sock danced in the wind. The plane swayed. The Messerschmitts were closing in with orange bursts flashing from their wings. Parallel explosions of mud and grass ripped the landing strip and raced toward Lucas. Patches of wing covering tore open, and the plane jolted. He had struck the runway. The plane bounced, landed again, and lurched left. With the left gear gone, the plane spun crazily. A carousel of trees, fence, and cows swirled around him. The left wings crashed into a giant conifer and sheared off, and the plane vaulted into a ditch and slid to a stop. The vultures zoomed past and started to circle for another pass. A deafening explosion stabbed Lucas's ears. An orange fireball engulfed his head and the world went dark. Smoke choked him. He couldn't breathe or see. He tried to scream, but the hot wind burned his mouth, and no sound came out.

A shadow of a man swept by him, and somewhere in this dark, burning hell, he heard, *"Abel. Abel. C'est Emile. Vite. Vite."* Abel, it is Emile. Hurry. Hurry.

12

Lucas awoke in darkness. He remembered the explosion, the orange fireball, and his eyes burning. He'd closed them, but the heat had pierced his eyelids like a blazing sword.

Who was the shadow calling Abel's name?

The heat was gone now, but a thousand needles pricked his face and hands. Where was he? He blinked open his eyes, but saw only bizarre purple shapes swimming in a midnight-black pool: circles, squares, lines, and blobs that exploded like shooting stars into smaller purple ovals that bounced toward the periphery and disappeared. He strained to see, but there was no light. When he moved the fingers of his right hand, they felt as though he was holding a knife's sharp edge. He turned his head to the left—still no light. He moved his left hand, and the pain was less. He blinked again, and the black pool changed into a gray mist, like the clouds that swallowed the plane. He raised his right hand to his face, but he couldn't feel his skin. He tried with the left, but there was still no feeling.

He crossed his arms and ran the right one down over his left hand and felt a gauze boxing glove. He reversed sides and felt a bandage the size of a melon on his right hand. He drew his right forearm over his eyes and felt the patches. His heart raced and his breath came in jerks. His chest felt like heavy stones were stacked on it. He tried to scream, but his mouth was too dry to make a sound. Panic enveloped him. Images of home popped into his head: Erika in their hotel in Grinzing, Edouard at home, his mother's headstone, the envelope, Schrader dying. He pulled against his soft restraints.

He raised his head from the hard pillow, but there was still only darkness. He swung his right arm to the side and knocked over a metal object that clanged on the floor.

A door squeaked and he heard muffled voices. Two men spoke rapid-fire French, and a girl spoke in German-accented English, "Let me go to him." Soft footsteps started toward him, and closer became a dull flapping sound as if the wearer's shoes were too big. He tensed every muscle in his body and felt as though his chest would burst. He couldn't breathe. Was he blind?

The kind German voice said, "Lucas, you are safe. We will take care of you."

He shook his head and raked his dry tongue over cracked lips.

"Would you like some water?"

He nodded.

A gentle hand lifted the back of his neck, and he felt the cold rim of a tin cup on his lips. He gulped cold water, gagged, and broke into a paroxysm of coughing. He lifted his head higher, trying to breathe.

She held his head and blotted the sides of his mouth with a moist cloth. "Slowly, don't choke."

He tried again, got two swallows down, and dropped his head on the pillow, exhausted. He wet his lips with his tongue. "Where am I?"

"You are in Gratwein, in a safe house."

"Abel?"

"He's safe. He was shot, but the wound was superficial. He was knocked unconscious; very lucky, yes? You saved both your lives with that miraculous landing."

Lucas's mind raced. Who were these people? French Resistance, Resistance, Communists?

He said, "Who are you?"

The gentle voice said, "We are the Austrian Resistance, working with the French. We will care for you until you can travel." She touched his face. "My name is Petra."

He heard footsteps across the room.

Petra said, "The men who pulled you and Abel out of the plane are here."

A male voice with a French accent said, "I am Emile Marceaux, a friend of Abel, and this is Alain Dautreive. We are with the Maquis, but we work closely with your Resistance."

Lucas raised his right arm and whispered, "Thank you."

Emile said, "Our doctor, Herr Doktor Kandler, came and bandaged your wounds. You have severe burns on your hands and face. Your eyes were badly burned, too, but the doctor feels you will probably see again."

Probably? Lucas slammed his head against the pillow again and again.

He felt Petra touch his face again. "There now. You're going to be fine. You will see again. He is a very good doctor."

Alain said, "We are giving you sugar water in the vein. Soon you can have soup. I'll write the recipe for Petra to make it."

Lucas made small circles with his right arm as if to say big deal, and Petra laughed. "Whoopee! He has a sense of humor."

"The landing you made was quite a feat," Alain said. "The 110s don't often miss. We got you out before they made another pass and destroyed your plane. It burned to ashes."

Lucas raised his right hand in thanks.

Petra said, "You were unconscious for some time."

"How long?" Lucas whispered

"Four days. We're glad you woke up."

Lucas strained to lift his head from the pillow. "Where is Abel?"

"Do not try to talk," Emile said. "Abel will return in a few hours and can answer your questions."

Lucas drifted into a fitful sleep, and a carousel of visions swept his dreams: Erika, wearing the blue dirndl she'd worn at her *abitur* (high school graduation), running through a field of crocuses, her golden hair flying in the wind; a full moon over the Loser; the priest and Donner; his father standing by his mother's grave; his father, arms shackled, being led to a wall; then—nothing.

Abel returned in three hours and walked to the side of the bed. "Well, how is our ace pilot?"

"Are you all right? I thought were dead during the flight."

"Well, my brother, I would have been without your heroics. You have slept away another day. Let's sit you up. Petra made you a bowl of Alain's potato soup. We'll see how strong you are. If you can eat this, you're ready to get up."

From the doorway Alain said, "I heard that."

Petra said, "I am here, too, Lucas."

Her voice. Touch. Warmth. She made his soul smile.

Alain chuckled and held a spoonful of soup close to Lucas's face.

"That smells good. Thank you, my friend."

Alain said, "You are speaking better. Have all you want. There's plenty in the kitchen."

Lucas blew on the soup and sucked it into his mouth.

When he tried another swallow, the hot soup spilled onto his chest.

Petra hurried to the bedside. "Here, let me feed him." She wiped his nightshirt, and continued to spoon the soup to Lucas, pausing between swallows. When he was finished, she wiped his mouth with a wet cloth, and her fingers brushed his cheek just below the bandage.

Several days later, the doctor came. He asked, "How is our patient?"

Petra stood at the bedside. "He is trying very hard."

Dr. Kandler moved to the bedside, rolled up his sleeves, and slipped on rubber gloves. "Lucas, I'm going to remove your eye bandages. Your vision will be blurred for some time, but you should eventually adapt."

Lucas felt the bandages loosen, and the doctor gently pulled them off. He saw a blurred vision—the walls of his room and men's faces that he couldn't identify. And then he saw Petra. She smiled and blotted tears from her eyes. Lucas's gaze locked on her face, and he flashed back to the mine and the lady with an enigmatic smile.

Petra said, "There, can you see us? Your eyes look beautiful."

Dr. Kandler chuckled. "I think he likes what he sees. I'll call on you again next week. If you need me before then, send a message and I will come."

Lucas reached for the doctor's right hand. "Thank you, sir."

The room remained quiet as Lucas glanced from object to object and associated the correct name and face of Alain and

Emile. Alain had a mustache; Emile was bald. After a while, Alain and Emile left the room. Abel sat down in the corner.

Lucas sensed Petra at his bedside. After a bit, she placed her hand on his arm, and it calmed him. He dozed off, but awakened as he heard her walking away.

Abel walked to Lucas's side. "During the last two weeks, I have been working with the Maquis, getting more information from home."

Lucas jerked his head up from the pillow. "What?"

Abel squeezed Lucas's shoulder. "We were told your father was arrested and taken to Ebensee—"

Lucas slammed his head on the pillow and cried, "No!"

"It is not for certain. We have heard nothing more. He is probably still alive, but we cannot be sure. There is talk of organizing an escape attempt, but the camp is a fortress, and we don't have the manpower or arms. They may be holding him in one of the caves. Inaccessible. We'll do nothing without your approval."

"Erika?"

"She and her family were questioned and released. They are at home."

Abel sat on the edge of the cot. "There's something else."

"More bad news?"

"Yes. Father Messmer was questioned by the Gestapo, but not arrested. Our intelligence learned that the Nazis feared his arrest would trigger a mass revolt by the villagers. He is forbidden from leaving the church, and a guard is posted there to prevent his escape. Our agents asked for permission to visit him, but were denied."

"Is that all?"

"Afraid not. The SS arrested Herr Kogel and Karl at the airfield."

Lucas said, "Madness. Didn't they see the lump on Karl's head? I'm sorry, but I'm glad he woke up. Where are they being held?"

"In Munich. They'll be brought to Altaussee for interrogation. We are the fugitives." Abel paused and took a deep breath. "Kaltenbrunner has ordered that we are to be shot on sight."

"This is hopeless. We'll never escape. You should leave. Run. Go somewhere you'll be safe."

"Never. I won't leave you. And there are no safe havens."

"You would tell me to do that if you were hurt," Lucas said. "And I would do it."

Abel playfully slapped the top of Lucas's head and stood up. "Go back to sleep." He left the room.

Lucas thought of the envelope buried next to his mother's gravestone. *It could save thousands of lives? Will I ever get back and find out?*

For the next month, Lucas was confined to his dark room. His sight improved, and he was able to read by a dim light. Petra brought German classics from the library: Schiller, Goethe, and Gunter Gras. When his eyes grew tired, she read to him. He was unable to sleep and ran a fever from his burns for a few days, but the infection subsided with sulfa powder. Petra brought food for each meal and cared for his wounds. For breakfast, he ate what was left over from the night before. He nibbled at the food, trying to make it last until dinner, and the monotonous schedule repeated.

Petra took him into the courtyard in the evenings. They walked short distances at first, but one night entered a small copse of trees, and he sat down on a rock and looked at Petra.

"What is Abel doing?" he asked.

"I do not know."

She took his hand, and their faces were close. She leaned toward him, and he felt her warmth. Affection? Gratitude? Erika's smile danced through his mind. He pulled Petra to him and kissed her forehead. "I think we should go in now."

They returned to his room, and Petra made a pot of tea.

Abel burst in. "I have news."

Lucas leaned forward. "Father? Erika?"

"No. Sorry. We are invited to a joint meeting of the French and Austrian Resistance."

"That's dangerous."

"I've been attending their meetings. Everyone knows about us. The organizer wants you to come with me to the next meeting. They asked me to speak and introduce you. Everyone loves a hero."

"Why didn't you tell me what you were doing?"

"I didn't want to worry you. You have enough to think about, and I wasn't sure. It's an honor for us." He paused. "So, will you go?"

"What about transportation?"

"A member, who is a farmer, has a truck. The back is covered with a canvas flap." Abel chuckled. "We may have to hide under turnips."

"Why do you make jokes about serious situations?"

Abel braced his hands on his hips. "Give me an answer."

Lucas walked to a chair, sat down, and held his head in his

hands for several minutes. He finally looked up at his brother and took a deep breath. "Yes."

At 1700 hours on March 29, 1945, a dark-green truck with its lights switched off arrived at the safe house. The driver remained in the truck. Lucas and Abel ran out and slipped into the canvas-covered bed among boxes of tomatoes and turnips. Lucas peeked out and enjoyed the ride along the moonlit River Mur on the way to Graz.

They arrived at the Mueller Meeting House and entered through a side door. Inside was a large meeting room filled with men dressed in lederhosen, long black socks, and gray and green jackets. A microphone stood atop a dais at the front of the room.

Many of the men recognized Abel, and the hum of conversation stopped. Georg Becker, the Graz Austrian Resistance leader, greeted them and led Abel to a chair on the dais. He introduced Lucas to another officer, and they sat in the first row. Within twenty minutes, Wiederstanders (Resistance members) filled the space to standing room only.

Becker introduced Lucas to a thunderous standing ovation.

All the doors were closed, and guards were posted outside. After Becker recounted the story of their heroic flight, he introduced Abel, who walked to the microphone and raised his right fist. The audience rose to their feet and with riotous applause returned the Wiederstander salute.

Abel spoke in German, discussing glowing reports on their acquisition of small arms and ammunition. The German Sixth Army was retreating from the advancing Russians, who raped and pillaged as they moved west. Hitler remained in his bunker under the Reichstag in Berlin as Russian infantry advanced on the city. Stalingrad was still under Russian control. Food and rations for fighters in the mountains were lacking. He announced that advance patrols of Patton's Third Army had reached Munich.

Gunfire burst out in the hallway, the rear doors were blasted open, and six Gestapo henchmen stepped over the dead guards. Spinning and hissing white smoke, a Nazi grenade landed in the room.. A thunderous explosion killed all men in the last two rows and sent body parts flying about. Six more men in long black leather coats crashed in. Whistles screamed. Gunshots rang out. Chaos and panic ensued. Shouting, men raced toward the exits. Four were shot dead. Others were hit by the blazing gunfire and survived with hands raised.

Abel leaped from the dais and ran to Lucas. They dove behind overturned chairs. In the sudden silence, clicking boots approached. They crawled across the blood-splattered plank floor and hid behind a post. Three long black coats surrounded them, Lugers drawn. They were handcuffed and forced facedown onto a pool of warm blood. Lucas rolled over, and a Gestapo thug kicked him in the belly, jerked him to his feet, and pushed him and Abel toward thirty Resistance members, hands tied, huddled in the front of the room near the dais.

"Don't answer any questions," Abel whispered.

A Gestapo agent cracked him in the head with a Luger.

They were shuffled toward the back of a line of men. They watched and listened as each man, one at a time, was interrogated briefly and led through a side exit into an alley.

Two minutes after the first prisoner was led out, Lucas jumped—gunshots. The line moved quickly.

Nearer the dais Lucas saw a fat, red-faced Gestapo agent sitting at a table.

A Resistance member was dragged toward the Gestapo judge. After a brief questioning and being told he could live if he joined the Gestapo, the Resistance fighter shouted *"Nein!"* The agent pointed to the doorway leading to the alley. Gunshots followed.

This process repeated, and twenty-one men were sent to their deaths.

The agent who had struck Abel shoved Lucas forward. He stood before the Gestapo judge who sneered. "Name?"

"Kemp," replied Lucas.

"Papers?" chided the judge.

Lucas handed his forged papers to a young assistant who handed them to the judge. He read them, and a feral smile distorted his fat face. "Do you really expect anyone to believe these lies?"

"They are my legal papers."

"Well," said the judge, "come here before me."

Lucas stepped up onto the dais, hands tied behind his back.

The judge stepped close, and Lucas gagged on his foul breath. They stood eye to eye.

The judge shot his right hand over Lucas's left shoulder. "Heil Hitler."

Lucas bowed his head and said nothing.

Abel, standing next in line yelled, "He is telling the truth, sir."

A Gestapo agent slapped Abel. "Silence."

The judge continued, "Ah, so you have a comrade. What caused the burn scars on your face?"

"Automobile crash, sir."

The judge strolled behind Lucas. "Heil Hitler."

Lucas stared at the floor.

The judge screamed, "Say it, or I'll have you shot."

Lucas's face reddened. He spat in the judge's face. Everyone gasped, and the judge pointed to the exit door. "Take this slime to the wall."

Abel broke away and stepped forward. "He's a pilot. He can fly for the Reich. His father flew with the Luftwaffe in World War I." And in a proud voice, Abel said, "And I am a wireless operator."

Silence spread over the room. The judge held up his hand for the men to release Lucas. "Is that true?"

Lucas nodded and pointed to Abel. "He is an expert wireless operator, trained in Graz by the Luftwaffe."

The judge strutted back to the dais and sat down. He waggled his finger at Lucas and Abel. "You should be shot, but Germany needs men to fight, even criminals like you. So, I will give you a choice. If you refuse, you will be taken through that door, shot, and fed to the pigs. Or, I will give you both the opportunity to serve in the Luftwaffe. Of course, you must be trained, and we will find out if you are lying. If so, you will be executed. What is your answer?"

Abel said, "We accept and thank you for the opportunity to serve the Reich."

The judge stared at Lucas and raised an eyebrow.

Images of Edouard and Erika flashed through Lucas's brain. Bludgeoning grief. *My God, I may never see them again. Control yourself. What kind of plane will I get? Will we stay together? How can I avoid killing Allies?*

He scowled at the fat bastard Nazi. "I will fly."

13

Ebensee Concentration Camp

Edouard knew that Ebensee was one of the most notorious of the Nazi concentration camps.

Prisoners were used for slave labor to dig huge tunnels in the adjoining mountains to house the V-2 rocket factory.

A Nazi corporal had tied Edouard's thumbs together parallel to one another behind his back. His arms were then pulled up by a rope looped over a beam. He stood still as a stone. His shoulders felt as though they would be pulled from their sockets.

The questions and beatings had stopped, but he knew they would resume. He craned his neck to see over the shoulder of Bachmeier, standing at the window with his back toward Edouard. A giant elm shaded wild crocuses in the garden. Traun Lake glistened in the distance, mirrorlike, and Edouard remembered hiking there as a boy.

SS Commandant Hans Bachmeier turned from the window and strolled back to Edouard. He tapped his cigarette on a gold case and lit it. "Would you like a smoke? It might help you relax a little."

"Nein danke, Herr Hauptmann." No thanks, Chief.

Bachmeier leaned close enough that their faces were only inches apart. "We are asking only a simple question, Herr Brunn.

We're trying to treat you with the respect befitting an educated man. True, you have been misled in becoming involved with the criminals in your Resistance, but we are understanding and considerate." He suddenly stood straight and walked back to the window, drawing deeply on the cigarette and blowing a contrail of smoke. "But if you continue to refuse to answer our questions, we have other means to obtain the information."

Edouard did not respond.

"Where is your son?"

"I don't know. The last time I saw him he was at home. He was going to the abitur celebration with his fiancée. I've told you that over and over. It's the truth."

Bachmeier tossed his cigarette onto the plank floor and ground it with his boot. "Yes, you have told us, but you are lying. I know it; you know it. He went on a spy mission disguised as a priest. He killed a Wehrmacht guard and stole a priceless masterpiece. We know that he escaped, stole an airplane, and crash-landed at Gratwein under attack by Messerschmitts. Who does he know in Graz? Perhaps one of your university professors?"

"Maybe he died in the crash."

The Nazi threw up his arms in disgust, walked to the window, and closed the shutter. "Enough of this admiring the beauty of our fatherland." He turned to face Edouard. "Do you know that a brave Luftwaffe test pilot died today?"

Edouard wrinkled his brow and stared at Bachmeier.

"I'm going to share classified military information with you." Then in a conciliatory tone he said, "We have a secret weapon. A jet aircraft that will snatch victory from the talons of inglorious defeat." He snapped to attention and clicked his heels together. "Heil Hitler."

"I cannot respond to that salute. As a military officer and honorable gentleman, you must understand that."

The Nazi's face reddened, and his neck veins bulged. "You traitor. I will cut off your testicles." He stepped back, lit a cigarette, and blew the smoke in Eduard's face.

"Aren't you curious, Herr Brunn? As a man of science, you should he intrigued by an airplane that flies faster than the speed of sound. It will blow the Allied bombers from the skies."

"I don't know about jet aircraft. I know nothing of military matters except the ways your army has affected life in our village."

Bachmeier sneered. "Of course not. And neither do your fellow conspirators in your pitiful little Resistance. What was your criminal son doing in the mine, Brunn? You're going to be shot for treason. Do you realize that? I'm offering you a reprieve. Tell us where your son is and maybe we can find a way to spare your life."

Edouard bowed his head. "I don't know what you want of me. I've told you the truth. I don't know where my son is."

Bachmeier threw up his hands. "Do you have any idea how the test pilot died?"

"No."

"The wings fell off of his airplane." Bachmeier flailed his arms in resignation. "They came unglued. The wings are made of laminated sheets of metal that are bound to the fuselage with some braces and a special glue. The glue is critical to stabilize the wings. Can you believe it? We lost an ace pilot and a miracle jet aircraft because we ran out of the glue."

Edouard suppressed a smile. "Why did you run out of glue, Herr Hauptmann?"

"The RAF bombed the Farben chemical factory at Ludwighausen, which was our only source of this special glue. In desperation they tried another kind, but it was ineffective and . . . the wings fell off. You should have compassion for a test pilot. We have reviewed your record in the Great War."

Edouard closed his eyes. "I served Germany to the best of my ability."

"Ah, so you did, but only because you were inducted into the Luftwaffe. You didn't volunteer. You were busy being the university scholar, a chemistry scholar. We have even read your graduate thesis. He pulled a note from his jacket and read: "'Relative Metal Bonding Capacities of Epoxy and Cyanoacrylate Glues in Aeronautics.' Now, don't you think it strange that you say you know nothing about glue?"

"I am a simple chemistry teacher at Altaussee Gymnasium."

"But you don't deny that you previously worked at I. G. Farben chemical factory?"

Edouard grimaced and moved his shoulders to ease the pain. "I did have a menial position as an assistant chemist for a short time after I left the university. My main project at Farben was developing improved fertilizer for farmers. I didn't work on any project concerned with glue."

The Nazi sneered, "Then why didn't you write your thesis on fertilizer?"

"I thought the epoxy glues might have industrial use. At Farben I only worked on fertilizer."

"You just have all the answers, don't you? Have you heard of the Luftwaffe's Nachtsjager? The RAF fears this Night Fighter. It is wreaking havoc with their nighttime bombing raids."

"I have no knowledge of the Night Fighter, sir."

Bachmeier said, "We know that you were an ace fighter pilot." He opened a folder. "You flew a Fokker D6. Credited with four kills, all British Sopwith Camels."

"I used to fly, before this." Edouard raised his claw hand.

Bachmeier glanced at the hand with only a thumb and fifth finger, turned back to the folder, and flipped a page. "You were shot down over the Somme Valley. Ironic, don't you think? You, now a traitor, bailed out near the area where our Red Baron, Mittmeister Manfred von Richthofen, died a hero's death."

"He was a great pilot."

Bachmeier smashed his fist into Edouard's face. "You may not speak of this hero, you coward." He punched him again, harder. "Coward. Traitor." He stormed from the room, slamming the door shut.

Edouard thought of Lucas and what Bachmeier had given him as the only news of his son. Had he survived? He remembered the mission in the mine. No one had expected the photograph. Lucas should have found a way to abort the mission when the guard took his picture. Otherwise, he doubted that anyone was astute enough to recognize him merely because he wore brown shoes not usually worn by priests. Was there an informant? Certainly not the Resistance Committee or Father Messmer. Otto? Who really knew Otto? Did the priest check his background? Probably not. They were the only ones that knew Lucas was going into the mine that night. He was dressed as a priest. Even witless Otto might wonder why. He heard shouts and a dog barking outside the window.

Two Nazi guards burst into the room, undid the ropes, and jerked Edouard from his chair. They shoved him through the door, and he fell sprawled on the ground. A gentle breeze brushed his cheek, and he breathed in the scent of crocuses. Birds sang from the elms.

Another door banged open and soldiers dragged a tall, dark-skinned lad with ink-black hair, perhaps sixteen years old, to the base of the elm. His head hung down, face bloodied. The soldiers looped the rope that bound his thumbs behind him over a stout limb of the tree, and yanked his arms up behind. The lad's feet swayed a half meter off the ground. He jerked his head from side to side, and his brown eyes flashed fear.

Bachmeier walked into the garden. "So, Herr Brunn, we will show you how we deal with traitors of the Reich, especially Jews."

The guards jerked on the rope, snapping the boy's arms higher behind him. He spun around as on a gallows. Edouard saw that the boy's thumbs were bound parallel, like his. The boy screamed. Birds in the elm fluttered away. Two soldiers grabbed the lad and stopped his spinning. Bachmeier kicked the boy's groin, and he vomited onto the Nazi's shining black boots. Bachmeier spat into his face and kicked him again. The guards pulled the rope tighter, lifting the victim higher.

Bachmeier screamed, "Release Lord."

The guards ran to the fenced-in kennel and opened a large wire cage. A monstrous black and brown German shepherd sprang into the garden. Edouard jumped back as Lord clamped his jaws onto the boy's left thigh. Lord jerked his head from side to side. A bleeding mass of flesh fell to the ground. Lord gobbled it up. He next went for the boy's groin and ripped away his trousers, exposing his genitals. As Lord's fangs tore into the boy's genitalia, a garnet geyser of blood spewed forth, forming a red puddle on the grass. The soldiers released the rope, and the boy fell to his knees and toppled sideways.

A soldier pulled Lord away, snapped on his leash, and led him to his cage.

Bachmeier nodded to a soldier, who walked to the lad and jerked his head around facing the lake. He jammed his Luger into the base of his skull and pulled the trigger. Brains and shards of skull splattered onto the yard and the trunk of the elm. Guards hauled the bleeding corpse away.

Bachmeier screamed, "Feed the Jew to the pigs." He wiped his boots with a towel, tossed it away, and turned to Edouard. "We will talk again in one hour, Herr Brunn."

14

Lucas and Abel completed their training in the Junkers Ju 88 Nacht-jäger and were posted to the Wilde Sau (Wild Boar) Squadron, at Grimbergen Airfield, north of Brussels.

Their Night Fighter carried a crew of four: pilot, copilot, nose gunner, and wireless operator, who doubled as navigator. At first Lucas and Abel were not familiar with the Night Fighter's complex avionics, communications, radar, night flying, and upward-firing cannons mounted atop the fuselage above the pilot's seat. Copilot Captain Bernhard Jagermann, with more than one hundred hours in the Night Fighter, had assisted in Lucas's training and welcomed the brilliant young Austrian to the squadron. Abel mastered the radio system with ease. Their experienced nose gunner, Dirk Schulte, fast-tracked their learning.

In their drills, Lucas mastered their approach below and behind the target aircraft. When the tail of the target appeared on the gunsight screen, the cannons automatically fired until they had cleared from below. The guns were set to fire at the wing-mounted engines where Lancaster fuel tanks were located. Firing at the fuselage could explode the bombs, destroying both aircraft. The Night Fighters surprised American and British airmen and blew from the sky.

The day after their arrival, the Wild Boar Squadron was summoned for an emergency scramble. Eighteen men, including Lucas, Bernhard, Abel, and Dirk, sat in a large room with desk chairs, each with an ashtray. A large military map of the eastern coast of England, the North Sea, and Western Europe stood on a dais at the front of the room. The commander entered, and squadron members, in full flight gear, stood at attention and sat at his command.

Commandant Anton Streicher, pointer in hand, stood before the map. "Gentlemen, at this moment a stream of eight RAF Lancaster bombers, with eight Mosquito escorts, is over the North Sea. Destination: Dortmund-Ems Canal. Their target is a point where the canal branches into two streams in a village called Greven, near Munster. We expect the Lancasters to use a low-altitude approach to drop their delayed-explosion bombs. That will make your approaches and use of Schräge Musik (up-firing cannons) impossible.

"In order to stop the Lancasters before they reach their target, our projected intercept coordinates are here." He pointed to a large red letter X. "The coordinates are fifty-one degrees north, seven degrees thirty-eight east. This is twenty kilometers northwest of Munster at Greven, Germany. Distance from Grimbergen is 256 kilometers, fifty-two minutes' flying time. Write the coordinates down and appreciate the precision. A brave German agent in London paid for them with his life.

"The Lancasters must be destroyed at any cost before they bomb the Dortmund-Ems Canal. Do what you must; the Japanese use kamikaze." A hush fell over the room. "Your mission is vital to the success of the Reich. Destruction of this site would result in closure of the canal, paralyzing our import of iron ore from

Sweden and coal and steel from the Ruhr industrial district. In other words, your failure on this mission could cause Germany to lose the war."

Commandant Streicher paused. The squadron stood and snapped to attention. Seventeen right arms shot out with a collective "Heil Hitler."

Streicher glared at Lucas, whose arms were at his side. "Dismissed and good hunting."

Lucas's stomach churned, and he felt near puking. How could he continue this charade? He must not endanger Abel. He felt his father at his side. I will not quit, ever. I will die before saluting the madman Führer.

The squadron met fog and misting rain as they left the building for their aircraft. Lucas's crew climbed aboard a Kübelwagen. Lucas said to no one in particular, "This looks like a bathtub on wheels." No one laughed.

The Kübelwagen rumbled past four Night Fighters and stopped before their Junkers J24Y. They hopped off and walked toward their aircraft. As they climbed aboard, nose gunner Dirk Schulte said to Lucas, "It's not a good idea to not salute the Führer. You're asking for trouble."

Lucas grabbed his shoulder. "Forget the Führer. Here are your orders for this mission: do not—I repeat, do not—fire at the Lancasters. Aim away from them to deplete your ammunition."

Wide-eyed, Dirk said, "That is treason. We could be shot."

Lucas exposed the Luger on his belt. "If you hit a Lancaster, I'll shoot you. Understand?"

Schulte buckled in.

Abel heard the exchange. His eyes widened. His shy, nonassertive, lifelong friend had turned savage.

They lifted from the runway through dense cloud cover at

one thousand meters. Lucas looked to his left as the setting sun eased into the horizon, emitting a red streak of light across the bruise-colored cloud floor and lighting up his cockpit like a discotheque. He wondered if fire from a Lancaster created red streaks. He looked at the instrument cluster and set the automatic pilot to the intercept coordinates.

After twenty minutes Abel spoke into his microphone. "Base control advises that there are not eight Lancasters, but three streams of eight, a total of twenty-four. The lead group with an eight-Mosquito escort is approaching Bremerhaven. ETA target forty minutes. Your mission orders: maintain altitude four thousand meters; twenty kilometers before intercept point begin dive to one thousand meters and engage. Do not abort."

Only the whir of the Junkers Night Fighter's two engines broke the silence.

Lucas said, "Well, that's great. This is now a suicide mission."

Near the intercept point, Lucas dove to a thousand meters and called base control. "Base control, this is Hunter J24Y, approaching intercept point, visibility zero, fog and rain, no visual or radar ID of Lancasters. Request permission to abort."

Static blocked communication. Lucas repeated his message.

The static decreased, and he heard only two garbled words: "not abort."

Lucas turned to port on a heading back to Grimbergen.

Dirk screamed, "Bombers ahead and above, three hundred meters. Targets acquired."

Lucas yelled into the microphone, "Do not fire until my command. And I repeat: do not fire at target. Aim ten meters starboard. Understood?"

Dirk agreed and looked over his right shoulder. Lucas was aiming his Luger at the nose gunner's head.

Lucas fired his cannons ten meters starboard of the bomber and saw Dirk's tracers just inside of his. As they cleared the planes, Lucas manually fired his Schräge Musik into empty space and turned to headings for return to base.

Abel said, "We should make another pass."

Lucas didn't answer. Forty-five minutes later, they touched down at Grimbergen on IFR (instruments). They taxied to their designated space, killed the engines, and climbed out of the aircraft.

A Kübelwagen stopped next to the Junkers, and the driver called to Lucas, "Lieutenant Brunn, the commandant orders you and your crew to report to his office now. Please get in."

They rode in silence to the two-story administration building, got out, and entered Commandant Streicher's office. They stood at attention. Dirk, Bernhard, and Abel said, "Heil Hitler."

Streicher said, "Brunn, you could be shot for your actions on tonight's mission."

"Sir, as I reported over the intercept point, visibility was zero. For the safety of my crew, I fired the best that I could. To have made another pass would have been suicidal."

Streicher's face reddened. "You should have crashed into the bomber."

"Sorry, I couldn't do that. If I had been in a single-seat fighter, perhaps, but I couldn't intentionally kill my crew."

Spittle dripped from the commandant's mouth, and he raised both arms in rage. "You disobeyed my orders. You were the commanding officer; you should have destroyed at least one Lancaster."

Streicher turned to the others. "Do any of you have anything to say?"

Abel said, "No, sir. I concur with Lieutenant Brunn's statement."

Streicher said to Dirk, "Sergeant Schulte, do you have anything to add?"

Dirk said, "No, sir."

"Bernhard?"

"Nein."

Lucas stared out the window.

Streicher returned to his desk and sat down. "I am filing a formal complaint against you, Herr Brunn, for flagrantly disobeying orders and failure to complete a mission. This will be sent immediately to the Reichstag in Berlin. You are ordered to remain on base and forbidden from further flights. I am recommending that you be immediately transferred to a parachute brigade on the eastern front. Graf, Jagermann, and Schulte, you receive a warning only." He looked at the three flyers. "Dismissed."

Lucas shot his right arm with the other two, but did not say "Heil Hitler. Lucas and Abel returned to their quarters. Neither spoke for an hour.

Lucas said, "You should separate from me and join another flight team."

"Ridiculous. Would you leave me?"

"That's different."

Abel put his hand on Lucas's shoulder. "We should do nothing now. No decisions. Wait. This may all turn into nothing."

Lucas flopped onto his cot. "Let's get some sleep."

Just before sunrise there was a soft knock on the door.

Lucas picked up his Luger, walked across the room, and cracked the door open with the chain lock still engaged.

A stranger stared at Lucas's face and then at the photo he held in his hand. "Are you Lucas Brunn?"

"Yes. Who are you?"

"That's not important. This is for you." He handed a note to Lucas and walked away.

Lucas closed the door and returned to his cot. They both read: "You escape tomorrow 0930 on white laundry truck, Bergen Wascheri. Rendezvous point southeast corner laundry, 0925 hours. Laundry worker, a Maquis, will load laundry into back of truck and leave the door ajar. Climb in when truck moves. Talk soon. You will be safe, my brothers. Alain."

Abel recognized his signature from the soup recipe, and they remembered their Maquis friends in Gratwein. They tried to make plans, but could only pray and hope.

15

At 0758 hours Lucas awakened Abel. "It's time."

Abel wiped sleep from his eyes and sat up. "What time is it?"

"Oh eight hundred. I want to stop by the post office after roll call."

After dressing they slipped on their fur-lined flight jackets and strapped on their Lugers. They walked down the empty corridor and stepped outside across a snow-covered tarmac to the administration building. As they walked into the preflight conference room, the hum of conversation stopped.

Commandant Streicher burst into the room, and the squadron snapped to attention. A sergeant called the roll, paused, and looked up as he called Lucas's, Bernhard's, Abel's, and Dirk's names.

Streicher said, "Last night's mission was a miserable failure. We lost one aircraft and crew, but that Night Fighter managed to destroy one Lancaster. Major Rudolph Hessler and his brave crew, with all guns blazing, crashed into the enemy bomber. At that moment the Lancaster was on a course parallel to the canal, bomb bay doors open. The two aircraft crashed and burned on the canal levy. There were no survivors, but thanks to their gallantry and the weather, the RAF did no significant damage to the canal. It is still operative"—he paused for applause while staring at Lucas in the back row—"no thanks to Lieutenant Brunn. For failure to obey my orders, he has been grounded and confined to the base pending future orders from the Reichstag. I'm proud of the rest of you and the efforts you made under extreme conditions. And now, a moment of silence for our lost comrades." He read each name slowly. "At this time we have no scheduled scrambles for today. The weather is miserable across northern Europe." He paused. "Dismissed."

The squadron answered with a thunderous, "Heil Hitler."

The crowd dispersed into small groups. Lucas and Abel were first out of the door. They reentered their building and went to the post office. Lucas looked into his open box, grabbed the envelope inside, and ripped it open. It was from Erika's father. Lucas read each word as tears welled in his eyes. He wiped his eyes with his sleeve and put the paper back into the envelope.

Abel stared at him. "What?"

Lucas burst into tears and handed the letter to Abel. He read it and hugged his brother. "I'm so sorry. Maybe we can set up an escape. The Maquis will help."

"Impossible. No chance—not from Ebensee."

Abel stared into the empty mailbox, vainly searching for an answer.

Lucas gathered himself. "First we have to get out of here." He glanced at his watch: 0845. "Let's have some coffee."

As they entered the café, Abel said, "How about a slice of Austrian apple tarte. "I'd like that, but we'll be lucky to get black bread." Lucas glanced at four tables with eight chairs at each one, all partially occupied.

Lucas chuckled as they got their coffee and black bread and walked to the table nearest the door. Three airmen sitting there got up and left without speaking.

Abel wolfed down the tarte as Lucas scanned *The Squadron* newsletter's headline: "Heroism in the Reich," a tribute to Major Hessler and the crew who saved the Dortmund-Ems Canal.

Abel glanced at his watch: 0912. He nodded and without speaking they made their way to the laundry building, near the security gate entrance. At 0925 they hid at the southeast corner of the building. The white laundry truck sat at the closed gate, motor idling. The attendant walked inside and picked up the phone.

Lucas said, "That's it. Abort."

Abel's eyes were fixed on the security post. "Wait."

The guard waved to the truck driver and pressed a button to raise the gate. The truck turned into the laundry entrance and drove to the back. It turned around and backed up to the loading dock. A worker pushed two large carts filled with laundry bags and tossed them into the back of the truck. When he was done, he glanced toward Lucas and Abel, and nodded. The truck pulled away, and Lucas and Abel chased it and jumped in atop stacks of white laundry bags.

After ten minutes the truck accelerated.

Abel looked at Lucas. "Autobahn?"

They shared a congratulatory handshake.

The driver opened the sliding window to the cabin. "First stop forty minutes, Namur."

Lucas and Abel crashed onto the laundry bags and slept.

In Namur they met leaders of the Maquis of Ardennes.

Regional Maquis Chief Normand Broussard was dark-skinned, square-jawed, and heavy through the shoulders with a saber tattoo on the left side of his neck. Ink-black hair hung from his forest-green bandanna. He said, "Welcome to Namur," and nodded toward a smaller soldier to his left. "This is Henri Deauville, my second in command." All shook hands.

Broussard gestured toward a large tent set in the center of the compound and motioned for Lucas and Abel to follow. "Emile is my cousin and tells me you stayed with them in Gratwein."

Lucas said, "They saved our lives—until we were arrested."

"Is it true the Gestapo released you so you could join the Luftwaffe?"

Abel said, "Not exactly. We were allowed to join the Luftwaffe or walk outside to face a firing squad. So we trained as night fighters, but intentionally failed our first mission and decided to defect."

The chief laughed. "Difficult decision, no? Well, it is our pleasure to welcome you here. Let us know if you need anything. Oh, one other thing, we've heard rumors that a valuable portrait, probably the *Mona Lisa*, was stolen from the salt mine in Altaussee. Have you heard anything about that?"

Lucas said, "Only that the thief is a defected Nazi who probably works with Goering's art expert. Who knows?" He paused and subtly winked at Abel. "What's your situation here? Many Nazis?"

"Yes. The Ardennes forest hides the good and bad."

"What can we do to help?"

"Intelligence reports a Wehrmacht platoon bivouacked fifteen K from here on the way to Dinan. We would appreciate it if you would join our fighters who are going to pay a surprise visit to the Nazi vermin."

Lucas looked at Abel and they both nodded.

"Departure at 0500. Our armament officer will provide you with Berettas, grenades, and survival knives. I know you have Lugers, but you can never have too many weapons."

Lucas and Abel said, "Thank you."

Broussard said, "We are a relatively small operation of Maquis d'Ardennes. Your final destination is a safe house in Dinan, France. They will have plenty of work for you, or they can assist you in contacting the Americans, if you wish. So, have something to eat, get some rest, and sleep."

Abel waved. *"Bon soir et merci beaucoup."* Good night and thank you very much. They found their quarters—a small tent with two cots and a chair. Lucas flopped onto his cot and fell asleep right away, his Luger at his side. An hour passed, and he was awakened by a scraping noise. He sat up, pointing his pistol at the entrance. He saw Abel leaning forward in the chair, rubbing a shadowed object held between his knees.

Lucas lowered his pistol. "What are you doing?"

"Sharpening my survival knife."

16

At 0500 hours the next morning, Broussard greeted his platoon gathered around a troop carrier loaded with two bazookas. He raised his right hand and squeezed a toy clicker. The men laughed.

"Don't laugh; this toy could save your life. If you hear a strange noise close to you, click this device twice. Like this." He clicked it twice. "An all-clear answer is the same. The Americans used this at Omaha Beach." He looked at the clicker and smiled. "I'll bet this toy can speak French as well, no?"

He passed out the clickers as the men laughed and climbed aboard the troop carrier. Lucas and Abel sat on benches with four others in the canvas-covered bed of the truck. Three men sat in the large cabin with Broussard, the driver, and Deauville next to the right front window. They drove slowly because of decreased visibility and the hilly terrain. The dense forest encroached within one meter of the cracked asphalt road.

After travelling fourteen kilometers, Deauville pointed to a wide flat space at a sharp corner to the right that partially hid their truck from the road in both directions. They unloaded the bazookas and other arms and followed Chief Broussard into the forest, rifles at the ready. Lucas and Abel were toward the rear, just ahead of Deauville.

A high-pitched birdcall sounded. Broussard waved his right arm down, and they squatted, all eyes searching the area. Moments later they moved forward to a chorus of chirping cicadas that helped mute their footsteps as their trail started down. They walked slower facing into the wind.

A screaming airplane engine fractured the silence. The platoon dove for cover. Lucas looked up. A Messerschmitt 110 tumbled crazily from the sky, disappeared into the nearby forest, and exploded. Smoke smothered the platoon as they got back onto the path.

Broussard cried, "What was that?"

"A Messerschmitt 110. Notice anything strange?" Lucas said.

"There was no smoke or fire. No RAF Mosquitoes."

"The right wing was missing."

Broussard waved smoke away. "What the hell? We have a mission."

A Wehrmacht soldier lunged from the forest, his bayonet pointing at Deauville's chest. The small Maquis second in command dodged the thrust and grabbed the attacker's shoulders in a wrestling hold. As they fell Abel slashed the Nazi's throat. Blood spurted from the large neck artery, bubbling from a severed windpipe.

Lucas and other Maquis gathered around and made way for Broussard. The Nazi lay on his back, his body twitching, blood spurting and gurgling sounds coming from his neck.

For a few seconds, Broussard looked down at the lad, then

he pulled his knife and stabbed him in the heart. "Take his rifle and grenades. He's a peripheral guard. No need for him to suffer. There will be others." He jogged to the head of the column and stared at his men. "On guard." He waved for them to continue down the trail.

Ten minutes later Broussard stopped them again. He sent six soldiers to the left and four to follow him to the right: Deauville, Lucas, Abel, and a scared French lad, sixteen years old, who had soiled himself.

They approached an overlook and looked down on a cove with a small pond surrounded by four tents and three troop carriers.

Broussard said to Lucas, "What do you call this in a casino? Jackpot? There must be one other guard." He looked across the cove and saw his camouflaged compatriots. Broussard held up three fingers and received the same signal from the other side. He turned to Deauville to set up the bazooka.

Lucas belly-crawled forward to Broussard and Deauville. "What do three fingers mean?"

Broussard raised his eyebrows. "It means we'll count down from three and then hit them with the bazookas and grenades first; then, if they don't surrender, we'll shoot anyone alive. We will not shoot anyone who surrenders, and we'll not hit the troop carriers. They're probably loaded with weapons and ammunition." He paused. "Lucas, this is not your fight. This is your last chance to leave." Abel said, "Any fight against Nazis is ours."

Lucas looked at Broussard. "I'm not sure I can do this. Sorry."

"Understood. Stay to the rear and keep your head down."

Lucas lowered his head and slammed his eyelids shut. He rembered Horst Schrader kneeling on his chest, choking him.

Breathless, he felt the hunting knife in his hand and with a desperate thrust the knife sliced into the Nazi's chest, eyes widened, staring at eternity. Schrader slumped onto Lucas, who shoved him away. The vision vanished. His eyes flew open.

Broussard held up three fingers and counted down. When there was only a fist, the bazooka belched a white cloud as a dozen Nazis ran for their lives. An answering blast from across the cove killed six Nazis. Ten more ran from the tents, blindly firing machine guns.

Broussard fired the bazooka again as Deauville machine-gunned Nazis running toward the troop carriers. Abel and Henri hurled grenades. Another bazooka blast from the other side removed the remaining tents, a direct hit on seven Nazi soldiers. Bloody fragments of arms, legs, heads, torsos, and bowels floated in the pond, the water now colored black, saturated with Wehrmacht blood.

Broussard yelled, "Cease fire."

Black and white smoke enshrouded the pond and its garden of dead humanity. One surviving Nazi, hands raised, followed by ten other survivors, walked to the clearing next to the troop carriers.

Broussard said to the captives, "Throw down your arms and step back five paces." The Nazis complied, leaving a stack of pistols, rifles, grenades, and knives. "Search them," Broussard said. When the search was completed, finding no additional weapons, he commanded, "Tie them up."

Three gravely wounded Nazis writhed and groaned from the ashes of one of the tents. Broussard said, "Who is in command here?"

One man stepped forward. "I am."

"Name?"

"Uberlieutenant Wolfgang Mueller."

Broussard walked to him and spat in his face. "Well, Wolfgang, would you like to finish off your wounded comrades as you would if they were RAF or American flyers?"

"I follow orders of my superiors."

"Well that's the difference between human beings with a conscience and Nazi pigs who follow the orders of a madman." Broussard ordered two of his men, "Take care of them and make a place for them in the lead troop carrier." He turned to four other Maquis and said, "Search the troop carriers."

The Nazis were ordered into their own vehicles. Broussard assigned drivers and guards.

The remaining Maquis platoon, Lucas, and Abel formed a circle holding hands. Broussard said, "Would someone lead us in prayer?"

As a private said, "God be with us. Amen," a twisting Nazi grenade bounced into their circle, spinning white smoke and hissing. Men in the circle dropped hands and fell away. Henri Deauville fell on the grenade as it exploded. Once the smoke cleared, the others slowly approached the shredded mass of burning flesh, all that was left of Henri.

Lucas turned away and vomited onto the dirt.

No one spoke for several minutes. Broussard stepped forward and saluted the remains. He lowered his hand. "Here lies a hero. Collect the remains. He rides with us. They flinched as a gunshot rang out in the nearby forest. A Maquis soldier walked from the woods, his rifle slung over his shoulder. He looked at Henri's remains and said, "I found the other guard."

Broussard slapped him on the back. "Good work." He then invited Lucas and Abel to ride with him in the same troop carrier.

As they started away, a Maquis corporal came running to them. "Commander, we found arms, ammunition, and five hundred thousand French francs in the trucks."

Broussard said, "Ah, take that with us to headquarters in Dinan." He turned to Lucas. "So, you have seen how the Maquis fights evil."

Lucas bowed his head. "I wish I could explain. I feel so—"

"Forget it. We move on."

17

As they neared Dinan, the road widened, affording spectacular vistas of the River Meuse flowing through the Ardennes forest. Broussard slowed at the crest of a hill, and there before them was a spectacular view of Dinan, Belgium, the cityscape dominated by a towering citadel.

He pulled into an overview parking area, switched off the engine, and sighed. "After the grisly business of the morning, let's just relax a moment and enjoy some historical culture of one of the most beautiful cities in the world." He waved toward a notched pyramidal-shaped rock at the edge of the river. "Here stands le rocher Bayard (the Bayard rock). The notch atop this legendary rock was separated from the main rock by an explosion to create an opening for French troops of Louis XIV. However, legend has it that the rock was split by the hooves of a magical giant Bayard horse when it jumped over the River Meuse carrying the four Aymon brothers to save them from Charlemagne. When he jumped back, he fell in the river and drowned, but his magical powers saved him, and he returned to the Forest d'Ardennes to happily roam forever."

Lucas said, "That was some horse."

"I'll bet he was never saddled," said Abel from the rear seat, laughing.

Broussard glanced at his watch. "We must report to headquarters," he said and continued his tour-guide remarks. "The citadel is closed now, still surrounded by bunkers where German gun placements were before the Americans captured Dinan. A guillotine is still in the basement; I've seen it, a rather complex device. They murdered using firing squads and the gallows, which stood next to the guillotine. However, we must remember that the Maquis also played a significant role in that victory.

"Our headquarters are adjacent to the American building. They took over a small hotel."

They drove through bombed-out ruins and arrived at Maquis headquarters. They parked the two Nazi troop carriers at the bullet-scarred curb. Broussard said, "I see our compatriots have delivered the prisoners and cache of arms and money."

They entered a spacious room with white walls and hardwood floor. A large inviting couch embroidered in red, yellow, and black sat in the center of the room. Broussard stopped and sat on the couch with outstretched arms, as though he was caressing the fabric. "These colors are from the Belgian flag, a tricolor with vertical columns of black, yellow, and red. When the flag is raised, the black column is nearest the pole." He paused, relishing his moment of Belgian pride.

Mahogany tables and chairs arranged in conversation clusters rested on rugs matching the couch. On the walls of the remnants of the lobby of the Hotel Meuse hung pictures of the Charles de Gaulle Bridge and the street where he was wounded in World War I.

One of Broussard's soldiers came through a door next to the former concierge desk. He shook hands with Broussard and nodded to Lucas and Abel. "The prisoners are secured in the jail next door. The officials told us we may keep the weapons and munitions. They counted the money: 507,000 French francs. They will deposit it in their bank account for later distribution to our forces." He paused. "We told the commandant about our two new comrades. He is waiting to greet us in his office; it's just upstairs."

They walked up carpeted stairs with bullet-scarred white wood railing. The commandant met Broussard in the upstairs lounge area. *"Bienvenue, mon ami."* Welcome, my friend. They kissed on both cheeks.

Broussard introduced Commandant Armand Bourget to Lucas and Abel. "These Austrian gentlemen came to us after defecting from the Luftwaffe. It seems they chose flying for Goering over a firing squad, but deserted at the first opportunity."

Bourget asked, "Where is your home?"

"Altaussee."

"Ah, the site of the famous theft from the salt mine. Do you know if the *Mona Lisa* has been recovered? We heard that Kaltenbrunner tore the village apart searching for it."

Lucas nodded to Abel who said, "We learned of the theft, but we didn't know it was the *Mona Lisa*. I was told that the thief was a German who worked with Goering's art expert, who bought it for two million Deutsch marks for the fat one in powder-blue uniform. It initially hung in Carinhall, Goering's hunting lodge, but was stolen from there and sent to Russia. There are many rumors floating about."

Lucas chewed his lip to refrain from laughing.

"Well, I'm sure," Bourget said, "the Americans will find it when they recapture Austria. And we also learned of your escape and saw Kaltenbrunner's posters offering a generous reward for your capture. We are honored to meet you."

Lucas smiled. "It's our honor, sir, and we are fortunate to have met and fought with Commandant Broussard and his brave soldiers of the Maquis."

Bourget said, "We know you are not criminals, but you have become internationally famous as a result of false Nazi charges. In fact, the British Special Operations Executive (SOE) in London has notified all Allies that they are most interested in speaking with you. A Colonel Smythe of the SOE called me personally when they learned of your escape from Grimbergen. Do you know why they are so interested in you?"

"No idea," said Lucas.

"They said it was important and want you to call them as soon as possible. Here is the number." He handed a note to Lucas. "You may use my private office. Give the number to my secretary, and she will place the call for you. I hope the lines are open."

Lucas and Abel went into the commandant's office and asked the secretary to place the call. She tried, but could not get a free line. She smiled. "Please have a seat. Calls to the UK have been difficult of late. They will ring us when a line is open."

Thirty minutes later the phone rang; the secretary answered, handed the phone to Lucas, and left the room. He held the earpiece so Abel could hear.

A voice said, "Is this Lucas Brunn?"

"Yes, and my partner Abel Graf is also listening. I'll answer for both of us."

"Jolly good. My name is Colonel Carnaby Smythe, head of SOE's Foreign Agent Deployment Division."

"How do you do, sir? Why did you call us?"

Smythe said, "Well, straight to the point; I like that. I'd like your permission to read several statements to you and ask that you confirm or deny that they are true. Will you do that for me?"

Lucas glanced at Abel and shrugged. "We'll answer the best we can."

"Good, let's begin: you two are Lucas Brunn and—Abel Graf, is it?"

"Yes."

"Both natives of Altaussee, Austria; Brunn, you are a pilot; who is Mr. Graf?"

"Radio operator, sir."

"Brunn, you are familiar with the Altaussee salt mine that the Jerries call Depot Dora."

"I don't know the name of the mine."

"You entered the mine without permission; you discovered fine art stored in the mine; you stabbed a Wehrmacht guard."

"Yes, in self-defense."

"Thank you. You joined and later defected from the Luft-waffe."

"Yes."

Smythe paused. "Have you ever been or trained to be a spy?"

"No, but we've been involved in a lot of clandestine activities while on the run."

"Do you have knowledge of the theft of a priceless master-work from the mine?"

"We've heard the story."

"That's enough of that, Mr. Brunn. I've been trying to reach you to see if you would be interested in training as a covert British agent in our special school at Dorking in Surrey and, if you qualify, return to your native Altaussee as a spy."

"Absolutely, with one condition."

"And what is that?"

"Abel Graf is my lifelong friend and an expert wireless operator. I will go if he agrees and is allowed to go with me." He handed the phone to Abel.

Abel said, "I will. Yes."

Smythe said, "Jolly good, then, we have an agreement."

Lucas and Abel hugged, and Lucas asked, "What do you want us to do in Altaussee?"

"We'll decide that when you are near completion of your training, which, I must say, is quite strenuous."

"How do we get to London?"

"SOE will arrange an RAF aircraft to pick you up at Dinan and forward the schedule straight away to Commandant Bourget. Is there anything else for now?"

"No, thank you, sir."

"Good. Cheerio."

Lucas hung up and looked at his brother.

Abel said through tears, "Can you believe it?"

18

Lucas and Abel arrived on an RAF executive flight Z1124 at London's Stansted Airport. An unmarked SOE sedan met them, and after checking their IDs, the driver took them directly to SOE headquarters at Norgeby House, 83 Baker Street. An armed guard led them to a large wood-paneled room with cluttered, floor-to-ceiling bookshelves on all walls. Twenty-two workers stood around three six-by-ten-foot wooden tables stacked with books and folded maps. The surface of a larger table in the middle of the room was covered with another map of Europe with toy airplanes, tanks, and soldiers marking the progress of current campaigns. The personnel moved the markers about using long, forked poles cushioned with cork. On a large screen at the front of the room was yet another European map with color-coded pins identifying SOE agent insertion and current location points.

Carnaby Smythe sat in his office beyond a wide window affording a full view of the war room. He noticed Lucas and Abel and waved for them to join him. He tapped his curved calabash pipe on a square hand-carved oak ashtray with small carved oak leaves at the corners of the glass-lined bottom. He met them at his doorway and shook hands. "Welcome, gents. How was your flight?"

Lucas said, "Good. Bumpy over the channel."

"Usually is. We have a very busy schedule arranged for you, but first let's have some lunch and then you can begin with the clearance section."

Lucas glanced at Smythe's desk. "That's quite a pipe you have."

"Yes, it is one of my favorites. A continuous vice, I'm afraid. I started smoking a pipe as a teenager at Eton and found it a great comfort in university studies at Oxford. Been a member of the Pipe Club of the UK for years. Well, off to lunch."

Lucas and Abel followed him to a private lunchroom and endured boiled lamb and cabbage. After dessert of strawberries and milk, Smythe wiped his mouth with a white cloth napkin. "There is a matter that we must discuss."

Lucas and Abel leaned forward, elbows on the table.

Smythe cleared his throat and stared at Lucas. "Commandant Armand Bourget called me about a discussion he had with the Ardennes Maquis Commander Norman Broussard."

"What about?" Lucas shifted in his seat and glanced at Abel.

"Well, Broussard reported that in the midst of a skirmish with Nazi soldiers, you refused to fight. According to him, you said, 'I'm not sure I can do this. Sorry.' Did you say that, Mr. Brunn?"

"I did, sir."

"That greatly concerns me."

Lucas bit his lower lip, glanced at Abel, and then faced Smythe. "I understand your concern, but I assure you that I am now ready to fight—to kill when necessary—to complete our mission. My motivation? The Nazis arrested and have probably executed my father." Lucas paused and swiped away a tear. "They also arrested my fiancée. It's personal."

Smythe stood. "Sorry to hear about your father and fiancée; however, personal motivation may get in the way."

Lucas raised his voice. "Well, it was also personal when I killed a Nazi guard on a mission for the Austrian Resistance in the Altaussee salt mine."

Abel walked to Lucas and hugged him.

After a brief moment in the coffin-quiet room, Smythe extended his hand to Lucas. "I trust you."

Lucas shook his hand. "You can."

A female officer arrived and, after introductions, led Lucas and Abel to her office.

She was a diminutive lady wearing a British navy uniform. She had brown eyes and auburn hair pulled into a tight bun secured with an orange comb.

She said, "My name is Martha Ellsworth. I am a certified psychologist, and my job is to assess your mental health."

Lucas and Abel glanced at each other.

"My questions are structured to evaluate your mental toughness and ability to withstand German interrogation techniques. Mr. Brunn, you may answer for both of you. Mr. Graf, if you disagree, speak out. May I begin?"

They both nodded.

"Are either of you homosexual?"

"No."

She proceeded through many questions regarding family

history, health history, memorization capability, diet, sleep habits, sex life, hidden grudges, and Rorschach tests for their interpretations of various bizarre black ink images on paper. And lastly she said, "Two more questions: Would you be able to work with a team of agents? And could you carry on with the mission in the event of the death of one or more of your team members?"

"Yes."

"Have either or both of you ever killed a human being, and on this mission, are you willing to kill the enemy?"

Lucas glanced at Abel, who nodded. "Yes."

She snapped her file shut and stood. "Thank you, gentlemen, and best of luck. That is all." She walked from the room leaving them alone, wondering.

A young man dressed in workout attire took them to a gymnasium. "My name is Harry. I'm going to put you through some physical tests—nothing too rough, I'm sure you will do fine. Put on these shirts and shorts. Give your shoe size to the attendant. See you on the mats."

They returned and, for more than two hours, Harry graded them doing push-ups, sit-ups, rope climbing, defensive moves if attacked with knife or gun, and sprinting across the gym ten times and back. He checked their heart rate before and after and entered results on a notepad.

When done, Lucas and Abel leaned forward, breathless, hands on knees, and searched Harry's face.

Harry studied his notes and said, "Well done, gents. You've performed very well, especially considering you started your day in Belgium. Strong blokes you are." He paused. "See the housekeeping folks, and they'll take you to your rooms upstairs."

"It is hard to grasp the reality of this," Abel said as he slipped off his shoes.

"I could not have imagined a better situation. It gives me hope." Lucas rolled over facing the wall.

"Roger that."

They were awakened at 0600 and taken to the conference room. Carnaby Smythe showed them to their places at a large round table with ten SOE senior staff, some in uniform, some in gray and black suits, all chatting.

Smythe said, "Will the meeting come to order?" He paused for quiet. "Sorry for the early start. There's tea and toast on the buffet; please help yourself as we go along." He called on a gray-suited man across the table.

"Good morning, gentlemen. I'm Lord Henry Dallam, chief of the SOE credentialing section. Our first order of business is to assign aliases and credentials for each of you. After this meeting, we will take your photograph and arrange ID cards, Swiss addresses, passports, drivers' licenses, and SOE ID cards. I'll explain other details when your papers are ready." He sneezed and blew his nose with the handkerchief from his coat pocket. "Now, I've selected aliases for each of you. If you don't like them, we'll find more suitable names. You must approve and be comfortable with them as they are critical for your survival. You must become that person, with names and addresses for immediate family. Do you understand?"

"Yes."

"For you, Lucas Brunn, we have chosen the alias Major Hans Koenig, SOE ID number 05012934. Do you approve?"

"Yes."

"And for you, Abel Graf, we have chosen an alias Sergeant Karl Bonish, number 01051941. Do you approve?"

"Yes."

"Thank you, gentlemen. Your documents will be ready straightaway."

Smythe said, "Thank you, Lord Dallam. Now, for a new crisis. At 0517 this morning we received an urgent message from one of our Bristol coast observers. General Patton's Third Army and General Seidl's German Sixth Army are in a race to reach Altaussee, Austria. Reports from this alpine retreat confirm that the Nazis are storing their stolen cache of irreplaceable masterworks of art, statues, manuscripts, and gold in the salt mine. Hitler, in his Berlin bunker, has issued a Nero's decree, ordering the complete destruction of the salt mine and its precious contents. Many high-ranking Nazis as well as massive numbers of Wehrmacht troops are retreating to their alpine redoubt to make a last stand. Hundreds of Nazi troops have defected to the Austrian Resistance."

The members began talking all at once until Smythe called them to order.

"Prime Minister Churchill has approved all measures deemed necessary for the SOE to intervene," Smythe said. "We have here two young men who are natives of Altaussee and familiar with the salt mine and surrounding terrain, including the Salzkammergut. That will be an enormous benefit in selecting their insertion point. Major Koenig, who is a pilot"—he paused and looked at Lucas—"has been in the salt mine and observed an enormous hoard of priceless masterpieces. Sergeant Bonish knows the area like the back of his hand and is an expert wireless operator."

Smythe paused and looked at each member. "The floor is open for a motion."

The only female officer at the table said, "I move that we approve our two new recruits to train as British agents and parachute into the Altaussee area."

The room went silent until there was a second to the motion.

Smythe asked for discussion.

A bald-headed gentleman seated next to Lucas raised his hand.

Smythe said, "The chair recognizes the Honorable Stanley Wisher."

Wisher rose, wiping his glasses. "Thank you, Mr. Chairman. I realize that this is a crisis demanding immediate action, but don't we already have trained agents in Europe who can handle this mission? There's not time to train them adequately, and I fear for their safety—and failure due to their inexperience."

Another member said, "Question."

Smythe said, "A question has been called. Yeas?"

Most hands went up.

"Nays?"

There was one.

"The motion is passed." Smythe turned to Lucas and Abel. "Now, if you would please stand and raise your right hands for swearing in."

They complied.

Smythe read from a text: "Do you solemnly swear that you will do your utmost to complete this mission to the best of your ability, and no matter what the circumstance, will carry on, so help you God?"

They said, "I do."

"Meeting adjourned."

The members crowded around Lucas and Abel, using their new aliases in congratulations.

Smythe said, "Now, get your photographs taken and meet me in my office at 1000 hours."

They went to their quarters to relax a few minutes. Neither of them spoke until Lucas pulled out the clicker he'd gotten from Chief Broussard in Ardennes. "Let's not forget to take these babies with us." Abel reached into his pocket and showed his clicker.

19

Colonel Smythe hurried Lucas and Abel into his office, closed the door, and led them to a mahogany table with four chairs upholstered in a forest-green fabric.

"Your training schedule is formidable. Here it is." He handed them copies and read aloud, "Clandestine skills, hand-to-hand combat with guns and knives, demolition, camouflage, map reading, marksmanship, and parachute training. You'll start today at 1600 hours at Dorking in Surrey, fifty K southwest of London.

"You have reservations on a local train to Dorking at 1300. Take separate taxis at different times to Charing Cross station. You'll be seated in separate cars. Don't try to make contact on the train. No luggage. Change into the clothes in these cases. They are color coded so your handlers can identify you. Stay separated until you meet at the Dorking Training School."

Lucas said, "I can read maps, if that would help."

"Good," Smythe said. "Your instructor will give you a test. If you pass, time saved and you can help Abel. So, here are your identity papers and some cash." He glanced at his watch. "Now, off to your room, change, and don't miss your train."

Charing Cross Station was packed with men and women in various military uniforms. Lucas bought a London *Times* from a kiosk and made his way to his window seat, 20 D, in car 7. He'd not seen Abel since he left Norgeby House and thought that learning to wait might be the most difficult lesson of all. He covered his passport as he slid it from the case and held it between newspaper pages to read it: Koenig, Hans, Major; DOB May 8, 1923; age twenty-two; address Bertoldstrasse 1487, 67 Lucerne, Switzerland. His physical description was perfect, his photo blurred.

As the train pulled away from the station, he watched adjacent rails slide by his window. The train slowed at an empty field cluttered with rusted cars and trash stacked against a dirt bluff that fronted slums with peeling paint fit for a ghetto. Lucas thought, Ah, but the Queen has her palace.

A sudden explosion blasted the train from the tracks. The engineer slammed on the brakes, and they began to slide and tilt to the left. A second explosion made car 7 flip onto its left side. Smoke and dust filled the cabin as people screamed and climbed over seats. Lucas fell into the aisle. His case spilled open, scattering papers and cash into the aisle. He stuffed them and his passport into the case and crawled into the space between cars. From on top of the door to his car, he kicked the exit bar and climbed onto the roof of car 7. He frantically searched for Abel. The coal car was ablaze, and the train looked like a burning, twisted dinosaur. He looked at the rails below; it was at least a four-meter jump, but he had no choice. He leaped, trying to land between rails, but his right foot caught the side of a rail, severely twisting his right ankle. He tried to stand, but he fell. He looked toward the front of the train and saw other people leaping to safety. He started to crawl and finally managed to stand. He looked back at the station and limped toward it with excruciating pain in his ankle. He stopped to help a lady with a child who had fallen from another car. They could walk. Soon there was a tattered parade of people walking, many running, toward the station.

When Lucas reached the platform, he saw everyone moving in one direction. Searching madly for Abel, he followed the crowd and came to a stairway with an arrow pointing down to Bomb Shelter B. People pushed each other aside to be first into the shelter. Elderly couples huddled in corners, arm in arm. Husbands and wives shielded their children. Military personnel assisted civilians to find a place, most standing. Young and old were crying, wailing, and screaming. He scanned the large room for Abel. Then Lucas heard it: another cacophony of thunderous bomb explosions shook the wall, blasting plaster from the ceiling. People crouched, holding arms over their heads. Lucas stood near the center of the mass of innocent people whose next breath could be their last. Still no Abel.

The bomb blasts stopped twenty minutes later. Sirens sounded and red-coated Charing Cross personnel with bullhorns announced the all clear. They pleaded for people to "walk not run."

Lucas walked into the station to find madness. People were screaming at ticket masters, demanding a train. Damage was minimal inside the station; one kiosk was turned on its side with newspapers, magazines, and cigarettes spilled around it. Lucas picked up a city map and stepped onto the street to find even more madness. Dense white smoke mushroomed from a building at the corner, and falling debris prohibited safe transit. An ambulance, siren wailing and flashing lights ablaze, pulled up to a fallen man covered by a tattered coat. The emergency crew quickly checked the victim and loaded him into the ambulance.

Lucas leaned against the wall of Charing Cross; it was hot.

He spread the map open and searched for 83 Baker Street. Smoke choked him and blocked his vision. There were no taxis or city buses. Stores and pubs near the station were closed. He folded the paper under his arm and started walking to—he knew not where. Passing Bryman Road he saw lights down the street and walked toward them. The Lancer Pub was open and empty. He walked in, and after a while the barkeep appeared and gave Lucas directions to 83 Baker Street. A painful two-hour hike took him to a darkened Norgeby House with its front door locked. He stepped out onto the empty street and saw a light in a shaded second-floor window. There was no way to climb up. He searched an adjacent alleyway and found small pieces of red brick. He picked up a handful and began throwing them at the window. Finally, he hurled a half brick and shattered it. The window light switched off. Lucas waited. Shortly, a shadow came to the window. He whispered as loudly as he could, "It's Major Koenig." The shadow disappeared, and Lucas walked to the front door.

Colonel Smythe's secretary came to the door. "Major Koenig, thank heavens you're safe. You're limping. Where is your partner?"

"I don't know."

"I'll help you to your room and get some ice on your ankle. You need rest. I'll call the colonel straight away. He lives nearby in Kensington, twenty minutes away."

With an ice pack on his ankle, Lucas lay down on his bed, right forearm over his face. A kaleidoscope of the past few days' events flashed through his mind. He prayed for Abel and fell asleep. A few minutes later a knock at the door awakened him and Colonel Smythe walked in.

"Are you okay? Were you wounded? I hoped you'd have left before the raid. It targeted railway systems and water supplies.

Damn Jerry, they usually bomb only industrial areas." He paused. "I'll drive you to Dorking."

Lucas pulled his pants above the right ankle.

Smythe looked and said, "Good Lord. It may be broken. The ice should help the swelling." He reached to touch it, but Lucas jerked his foot away. "There's no way to get you to an emergency room. They're jammed all over the city." He paused and helped Lucas adjust his pants leg. "How did you get here?"

"I walked."

"Amazing—perhaps it's not broken."

"We must find Abel. I won't leave without him."

"Lucas, I know you two are close, but remember your sworn pledge to carry on with the mission no matter what happens."

"I know, but—"

He glanced at his watch. "We'll wait until 1800 hours. If he's not here by then, I'll drive you to Dorking."

Lucas sat down on the side of his bed and buried his face in his hands.

Smythe left the room.

A deafening, sucking sound filled the room, and Lucas dove for the floor. The outer wall exploded, spilling lumber and fractured building stones onto the wet street. Lucas rose to his knees. Dirty white acrid smoke choked him. He crawled to the doorway, rolled into the hallway, and slammed the door shut.

Smythe rushed up the stairway and knelt next to Lucas. "Are you all right?"

Lucas grasped the doorknob and pulled himself up. "I'm alive."

"My secretary died in the blast."

"I'm so sorry. She was just here and helped me upstairs. I wish—"

"I know. Come with me."

They walked into the street, heard small arms fire, ducked into an alley, and hid behind some large green trash cans lying on their sides. Sporadic gunfire continued, seemingly closer. They retreated farther into the alley and crouched in a dark corner. Smythe raised the lid on an upright boxlike trash bin. "Climb in." He helped Lucas scale over the side, followed him, and closed the lid.

A quiet veil of smoke covered the street. Amid foul-smelling garbage, total darkness, and fear, Lucas thought, *this ugly place may be my tomb.* He could hear distant footsteps that were moving closer. One person was nearby. Lucas's mind swirled with options: leap from the bin, shoot the intruder, lay still and pray, call out and hope. Then he remembered the Ardennes mission and Broussard's toy snapper. He removed it from his pocket and held it next to his ear. An eternity passed. He snapped twice and held his breath. Nothing. Then came the answering snap and the lid lifted from their tomb.

Abel looked over the edge. "Amazing." He helped Lucas and Smythe from the trash bin and playfully held his nose, shaking his head from side to side.

"Broussard was right," Lucas said. "They work."

The three men embraced and wiped away happy tears.

They searched the nearby area. "Did you hear the gunfire?" Lucas asked Abel.

"Yes. I shot two men who were setting fire to a building."

Smythe said, "Gentlemen, congratulations. You will make great spies. Now, it is time to get you to your training grounds."

20

Dorking in Surrey is a small market town in the valley of the Pipp Brook between the North Downs and the Greensand Ridge approximately forty-five kilometers southwest of London. Located between Box Hill and Leith Hill, Dorking features ten Georgian- and Victorian-style grand mansions. The SOE selected one of these uninhabited mansions, Wellesley House, to develop a Special Training School (STS) for cultivating prospective British covert agents. More than one hundred had been dropped blind into European countries, primarily Germany and Austria.

Colonel Smythe parked at the entrance of Wellesley House and switched off the engine. He said to Abel, "Help me get Lucas out. I'll get a wheelchair."

Lucas sat up and studied the ornate mansion. Was he dreaming?

Smythe and a personnel handler returned with a wheelchair and helped Lucas from the backseat. The handler made a note of their clothes.

"They are the correct color." Smythe chortled. "Damn difficult to manage during a bombing raid."

The handler laughed. "Jolly good, sir." He rolled Lucas into a reception area where Smythe introduced Lucas and Abel to a member of the senior staff. "This is Sergeant Richter, chief of inter-rogation techniques."

Richter said in a harsh German accent. "Name?"

Lucas stuttered. "Uh—Major Hans Koenig."

Richter smiled. "I planned to start your training on arrival." He glanced at Lucas's ankle. "You are in pitiful shape and will need some days off before we can begin." He turned abruptly and walked away.

Smythe frowned and said to the handler, "Show these men to their quarters and help them get settled."

Four days passed. Lucas adapted to his crutches and followed Abel about Dorking.

Richter met them in a hallway. "Throw away those sticks and come with me. Crawl if you have to."

Richter led Lucas and Abel into a darkened room with two chairs. "Sit there. Hands behind." He looped a black plastic band around their wrists and pulled it tight. The room went pitch black and a blinding white light flashed onto Lucas's face.

Richter shouted, *"Wo kommen Sie?"* Where are you from?

Lucas stared at him. *"Ich wer im Lucerne geboren."* I was born in Lucerne.

"Ah, so you speak German. Where did you learn that?"

"In school."

"What school?" The questions came in rapid-fire order.

"Berghoff Academy, Lucerne."

"What was your mother's first name?"

"Gretchen." No hesitation.

Richter proceeded to badger Lucas and Abel for an hour with

probing questions about family addresses, where their parents went to school, names of their gymnasium teachers, school friends, and on and on. Then he stopped abruptly and asked, "Where is your mother buried?"

Lucas swallowed hard, and his heart cried. He lied, "St. Gabriel's Cemetery, Lucerne."

Then Richter grabbed Lucas's right ankle, squeezed hard, and got right in his face. "Who is your best friend?"

Lucas grimaced "Abe—" He stared at Richter. "Edouard, my father."

Richter switched on the lights, placed his right index finger against his temple, and pulled his trigger thumb. "You're dead." He released their hands as Smythe came into the room.

Richter said, "He barely passed his first test." He turned to Lucas. "I questioned you now because you are still in sad shape, just as you might be in the field. You will have other surprise interrogations as you go through your training."

Lucas, Abel, and Colonel Smythe went to the dining hall, where they talked with some of the other recruits.

A crew-cut blond and blue-eyed lad from Munich introduced himself as Franz Gunther. "We're happy to have you here; counting you two, we now have twenty-four Bonzos."

"Who are Bonzos?"

"We are—all the agents. I have no idea where the name came from. Someone who was probably drunk made up a name for the recruits. Brothers, all for one, you know. You'll meet great men here. All are anti-Nazi, including a few of us, like me, who defected from the Wehrmacht. What's your story?"

"We defected from the Luftwaffe," said Lucas.

"Pilots?"

"I'm a pilot." He nodded toward Abel. "Karl is a wireless operator."

"I was a sergeant in the Wehrmacht who replaced our original platoon leader who was killed. Hitler gave us no food, guns, or ammo. We decided our Führer was a madman, and the entire platoon defected to the Maquis." He looked away and then back at Lucas and Abel. "It's nice to meet you. I only have three days left and then get an assignment. Good luck."

For the next three weeks, Lucas and Abel underwent extensive training in marksmanship, demolition, camouflage, tactics, concealment, hand-to-hand combat, map reading, and finally parachute training at an airfield near Manchester. SOE required Lucas to make only one jump because of his ankle. He made the jump successfully and returned with Abel to Dorking.

On April 1, 1945, at 0800, SOE STS, Dorking in Surrey, Colonel Smythe sat with Lucas and Abel in the Dorking administrator's office. The door was locked, and the mahogany shutters were closed. On one of the wood-paneled walls hung pictures of agents who had successfully completed their missions, including locations and dates, and returned to England. On an adjacent wall hung pictures of agents who died in their attempt to help crush the Nazi regime. There were two pictures of RAF aircraft used in inserting the agents, with names of the crews. The largest picture showed an RAF Halifax T for Tommy heavy bomber flying over snow-capped mountains.

Smythe said, "Congratulations, gentlemen. You've completed your training and are ready for your assignment. All that in only three weeks. I want to personally thank you for the critical information you've given to SOE. That data will help future missions to succeed. I now remind you of your sworn pledge when SOE approved you for training. Do you have any second thoughts or wish to withdraw?"

They both answered no.

"The name of your mission is Operation Ebensburg. Today at 1400 hours you will be flown to Maryland, the SOE base at Bari, Italy. You will receive additional critical training there, and soon, at a date to be determined, you will fly out of the RAF airbase at Brindisi, Italy. Your final orders are subject to change. You will be briefed prior to takeoff. And now, the details of Operation Ebensburg: one, you'll investigate the status of Depot Dora, the Nazi code name for the Altaussee salt mine repository, and determine if art is stored there. If so, assist in its protection from destruction. An American regiment, the Monuments Men, may assist you.

"Two, you'll organize the local Austrian Resistance and gather intelligence on recent Nazi troop movements, including evaluation of recent explosions at Toplitzsee.

"And three, you will capture or kill Obergruppenführer Ernst Kaltenbrunner and any other high-ranking Nazis reported to have retreated to the area. If possible, take all German prisoners alive. Accept Nazi military personnel who wish to defect.

"Good hunting, gentlemen. That is all."

21

At 1600 hours, on April, 1, 1945, Lucas and Abel arrived at the SOE base, in Bari, Italy, via a Halifax T for Tommy heavy bomber, the same type of aircraft that would take them to their drop zone in the Salzkammergut. The crew of seven, who called agents to be dropped Joes, knew nothing of their mission, but they answered their sometimes probing questions about jump procedures just before and at the P-hour, the exact designated time when they would leave the aircraft

The first officer said, "The aircraft is not pressurized. You must wear your oxygen mask at all times. You never know what might happen."

Lucas said, "Even at low altitudes?"

"It's the rule—all the time. And be sure your other Joes understand that. If they disobey, it could cost them their lives."

Abel asked the communications officer, John Morrison, "Are communications secure on flights from SOE Bari into the Salzkammergut?"

"It depends on altitude, temperature, and quality of wireless operations."

They were shown the large circular trapdoor in the floor of the aft fuselage that covered the opening through which they would drop.

The discussions and questions seemed random and casual, flyer talk, but the new Bonzos gained invaluable experience being inside the aircraft rather than looking at thousands of pictures and diagrams in Dorking training manuals.

They touched down and were met by the SOE base chief, Evan Clarke, who took them to a meeting room in the administration building. He made small talk for a while describing the facility and operations.

Lucas interrupted, "How's your weather been?"

"Mostly overcast but with fair to good visibility. The powers that be haven't given us the go date, but it shouldn't be more than a few days to a week. There are technical procedures that we must go over with you, but there's time for that. I suggest we show you to your quarters; mess is at 1800 hours. We'll meet you here tomorrow at 0800." He took them to their private quarters and said good night.

The new Bonzos sat down in overstuffed chairs, took off their shoes, and stared at each other. Lucas said, "It would have been tough to land a Halifax at Gratwein." They both laughed and changed for mess.

Next morning at 0800, Lucas and Abel entered the conference room to find Chief Clarke talking to a man dressed in hiking gear.

Clarke said, "Gentlemen, this is Jon Hermann, your alpine guide—"

Lucas interrupted. "We don't need a guide. Our orders didn't mention one."

"The guide is my order. You will find Jon to be an asset to your mission."

Hermann stood as Clarke introduced Lucas and Abel with their aliases. They shook hands and sat down as Clarke spread a map of Salzkammergut on the table.

Clarke said, "Jon will describe the terrain of your drop zone and escape routes. His native language is Italian, but he also speaks excellent German, English, and French." He nodded. "Jon?"

The guide tapped his left index finger on a specific point on the map. *"Ihr Zielgebeit ist am Zinken Hochebene."* He looked at their confused faces. "Oh, sorry."

Clarke said, "He said, 'Your drop zone is on the Zinken Plateau.'"

Embarrassed, Jon said, "I am sorry. I will speak English. This map is most important. Take a copy and put it in your memory. Okay?" He relaxed and immersed himself into giving understandable information. "This time of year, you will land in deep snow."

Lucas said, "Jon, your English is excellent."

"Thank you. I spent a year in Switzerland learning mountain climbing, and all the instructions were in English. So I had to learn fast." He paused. "The first problem after landing is finding equipment boxes. Then we must bury our parachutes. Very important. The Wehrmacht will hear our plane and post patrols with dogs and block all trails down on mountain.

"You must use spike shoes for rock climbing down the side of the mountain. It is . . . how do you say . . . like ice. Easy to fall. Stay away from Feuerkogel near our drop zone. It's a special camp." He put his index finger to his temple and pressed his thumb down like a trigger." He paused. "You understand?"

Lucas, said, "Concentration camp. Right? Thank you for warning us about the drop zone."

Jon rose, shook hands with them, and said, "Thanks, I see you later."

Lucas asked, "What do you know about Jon?"

"He's thirty years old, from a good Bari family. He's been around for years, leading tours, mountain climbing, and hunting. Never been in any trouble. Hates Nazis. We've thoroughly vetted him."

Lucas held up his arms in resignation. "We can still abort the mission."

Abel said, "Don't do that. Not now. I think he will be fine."

Lucas laced his fingers behind his head and thought. "All right, but we'll have to keep a close watch on him."

"Good," Clarke said. "Now, some good news. Our go date is tomorrow, May first, briefing here at 2300 hours, take off 0055. Target acquisition 0257, P-hour 0300. Now, I'd like you to spend some time with our mapreaders to go over peculiarities of the drop zone terrain. Shouldn't take more than a couple of hours, then you're free until the briefing. Try to relax and get some rest. Our prayers are with you."

That night Lucas and Abel entered the briefing room at 2300. Clark stood in front of the room facing seven airmen and Jon. He introduced Lucas and Abel to their flight crew, including the pilot, Officer Lowry Douglas.

Douglas said, "I want to introduce you Joes to the guy who is responsible for getting you safely out of the aircraft, lieutenant John Morrison."

Morrison waved.

Clarke said to the crew, "Gentlemen, these two men, Major

Hans Koenig and Sergeant Karl Bonish, are on one of the most critical missions in the war. Their alpine guide is Jon Hermann. You've been briefed on your route so let's get to it. Crew will ride to the aircraft as usual. Hans, Karl, and Jon will ride in back of a covered truck. The truck will back up to the plane so they can exit without being seen. Is that clear?"

All nodded.

"One more thing: the jump order is: first, Jon; second, Hans; last, Karl. Are there any questions?"

Lucas stood, "My orders stipulate that I am to be first to jump. I respectfully request that we follow those." Silence veiled the room.

Clarke chewed on his lower lip, pensive. "Okay, then. So be it, and Godspeed to all."

The crew and Bonzos rode to the aircraft and climbed aboard as instructed. Hans and Karl buckled in to seats on opposite sides of the drop trapdoor in the aft compartment of the plane. Jon sat next to Lucas. They pulled their heavy, green, fur-lined coats around their necks. Jon wore only a wool shirt with his jacket on his lap. All donned their oxygen masks.

They lifted from the runway at 0055 and banked to the northwest. Lucas looked through his porthole and saw beyond the right wingtip a full moon pasted onto an ink-black sky. He was strapped in to close quarters, shivering from the cold, and couldn't hear his own voice against the thunderous roar of the four engines and vibrations of the airplane.

Sergeant John Morrison, the wireless operator, handed them headphones. Pilot Lowry Douglas was speaking. "We're on a northwest heading parallel to Italy's northern coastline. At Ascona we turn north on a route east of Venice and on course to your DZ. Hope you Joes are comfortable in these luxurious trappings. Sorry the furnace isn't working. Be sure your oxygen masks are on and secure. You've got about two hours. Go to sleep. We'll wake you when it's time. Tallyho."

Lucas and Abel crossed their arms and leaned against the hard leather headrest. Jon was already asleep.

Lucas dreamed of his father, a brilliant chemist, a great teacher loved by his students. *A good father, but I would give anything to have five minutes to talk to him and tell him I love him. Then I would listen and wait;* Erika danced before him, her red, green, and blue dirndl skirt flying, graceful legs extended. Then they stood by their favorite elm in her yard, carving initials, but the bastard Kaltenbrunner came and stole Erika and the knife.

He came half awake, punching the air.

Abel screamed, "Wake up. What are you dreaming about? You are talking crazy."

Lucas straightened in his seat and looked at Jon, fast asleep.

Suddenly, the aircraft was rocked by a heavy explosion. Flak, and lots of it, exploded around them.

Morrison said, "Looks like Jerry knows we're coming. Assume brace position. Keep your masks on."

Jon awoke, panicked, ripped off his oxygen mask and restraining belt, and stood up, only to slam against the bulwark of the fuselage and fall to the floor. His face turned blue. He gasped for breath and lost consciousness.

Sergeant Morrison rushed to him, put on his oxygen mask, and when he woke up, slapped him across the face. "You keep the mask on. I won't do this again."

The flak intensified and flames burst from the inside port engine. The pilot shut it down and they nosed into a steep dive.

Morrison said, "We're lucky. No fighters. Yet. If we can get low enough, their radar won't work, and we may get out of this."

Pilot Douglas's voice came over the intercom. "Okay, Joes. We've been compromised. There may be a security leak. I think I can fly us out of here. You can abort the mission or jump. But I must tell you you're jumping into a shitload of Jerries. Your choice. Decide now."

Lucas glanced at Abel. They both nodded. "We go."

"Altitude thirteen thousand, P-hour four minutes. Check weapons, gear. Parachutes on."

Jon screamed, "I cannot go."

Lucas shook him. "You go with us. That's an order."

Morrison pulled Jon from this seat and secured straps and clipped his parachute static lines to the D ring welded to the fuselage.

Continuing their descent, the bomb aimer opened the bomb bay doors and released three canvas-covered equipment containers into the black night. The tail gunner watched three parachutes open and float toward snow-capped peaks. Under their jumpsuits, Lucas, Abel, and Jon each wore heavy civilian clothes and spiked boots to navigate the rugged mountainous terrain. Armed with fighting knives and Beretta pistols in their jumpsuit pockets, they tightened the straps on their parachute helmets and slipped into the harness.

The plane banked left and flew in a circle again, lining up on course to the drop zone. Morrison stood Lucas on the starboard side of the trap door, Abel and Jon on the port side. He removed the trap door. A blast of whistling cold air blew in, and the jumpers were blown against the fuselage. Morrison raised his right arm, listening to his headset.

The green jump light flashed on. Morrison tapped Lucas's shoulder. "Go!" Lucas disappeared through the opening. Morrison gave a thumbs-up. Jon froze at the hole. Abel grabbed his shoulders. "We need you. We will be okay." Jon closed his eyes and fell from the aircraft. Abel followed.

Lucas tumbled through the black, icy sky. His parachute snapped open, jerking him sideways; through his iced goggles, he saw forest, mountains, snow, and rock, but he was moving horizontally, being blown away from the DZ. Four minutes later he could see no visible landing area. His heart raced, and he scanned the blackness looking for Abel and Jon.

As he neared the tree line, he saw flashing lights in the forest. Nazi patrols. He floated below the level of the highest peak and maneuvered his chute to avoid trees. The trees vanished and a barren flat zone surrounded by sharp boulders zoomed up at him. He jerked his control lines and threw out his legs. He zipped past outcroppings of daggerlike rocks. As he crashed into the snow, he twisted his right ankle as a Tyrolean avalanche blinded him. He rolled over, wiped his goggles, and looked about. Nothing. He looked toward the sky, hoping the moon would illuminate Abel's and Jon's chutes. The moon was gone.

He listened and heard only the wind and distant barking dogs. After rolling up his parachute, he limped behind a rock, dug a hole, and buried it.

Back in the clearing, Lucas snapped his clicker twice. No response. He heard footsteps in the snow coming from behind a large rock. He aimed his Beretta, and Jon appeared, toting one of the equipment containers.

Jon asked, "Where is your radio man?"

"Not here yet. Did you find any other containers?"

"No. Probably buried under snow. I could see only half of this one."

They took their jumpsuits off and buried them. Lucas looked around and studied his compass trying to get his bearings. They walked fifty meters to the precipice of a high ledge.

Below were the lights of a village. Jon looked, grabbed Lucas's sleeve, and stepped back. "Feuerkogel."

Lucas understood, and they hurried back to the landing zone.

They heard barking dogs and garbled German shouts coming closer.

Jon pointed. "Nazis. Two hundred meters. We must hide."

They buried themselves under snow and waited. Lucas prayed for Abel. The barking dogs moved closer, fifty meters, and suddenly someone yelled a command. The Nazis and dogs disappeared.

They emerged from the snow, dug out, and opened the container. Lucas pounded the snow with his fist.

"What's the matter?" asked Jon.

"Our wireless set's not here. We have to find it; it's our only contact with Bari." For half an hour, they searched the surrounding area, looking up into trees and behind rocks. Lucas suddenly held up his right hand and listened. He heard the clicker, twice. He answered and ran toward the sound. Behind a rock, covered with snow, Abel leaped up and jumped into Lucas's arms.

"I thought I was a dead man. Did you hear the dogs?"

"Yes, but we learned about more than dogs." He pointed toward the east "Over that ledge is Feuerkogel." He made the motion of shooting himself in the head. "Understand?"

Lucas read his compass and studied the mountain range. "Something's not right." He looked back at the ledge. "My God, we're not on the Zinken Plateau. We're on Hell Mountains."

"What?"

Lucas studied the map. "Here it is on the map. Höllengebirge. We've had it. No one has ever scaled down this monster."

Jon said, "Ah, you mean the Devil Mountain. It's not so bad. I know it. We won't use the regular trail. The Bosch will block it. We must go down the side of the mountain." He pointed to their spiked boots. "Come, I show you."

Lucas said, "Lead the way."

22

Halfway down Höllengebirge, Jon stopped and raised his right hand. He crawled to the edge and looked down. Then he stood and walked to Lucas and Abel.

"Do you know how to rappel?"

They stared at each other, and Lucas said, "No, and I don't think this is the place to learn."

"It is easy." Jon motioned and walked toward the edge. "Come. I will show you how."

Abel said, "Is there a way to walk around to the bottom?"

"No. It would take too long. You could freeze." He pointed to the ledge. "It is only one hundred meters to the bottom. You can do it."

Lucas's heart raced; he could feel his pulse pounding in his head. He stared at Abel for the longest time. "What do you think?"

"I don't know."

Lucas said to Jon, "Let's have a look at the gear."

Jon opened his extra backpack and removed loops of rope, canvas straps, and metal hooks. Lucas and Abel followed him to the edge of the adjacent forest where he looped and secured a canvas strap around the base of a large tree trunk.

"This is our anchor. Do you understand?"

They nodded.

He held up an oblong metal ring with one spring-hinged side. "This is the carabiner. It connects the rope to your body."

Lucas said, "Just put the harness on me and let's do it."

Jon hooked the harness on Lucas and backed him to the edge. "Hold the right hand rope up high. When you want to descend, loosen it here." He pointed to a hinge brake. "You can't fall. When you get down, jerk the rope twice. Okay?"

Lucas backed to the precipice and looked over his shoulder. He stepped over the edge and stood straight. Relaxing the brake, he easily took a step down. He got into a rhythm and rappelled down the sheer face of the Höllengebirge. When on level ground, he jerked the rope twice, then stood in amazement as Abel rappelled down followed by Jon.

The three of them standing together, Lucas said, "How do you get the rope down?"

"We leave it here," Jon said. "I know I told you that Feuerkogel is very dangerous, but it is our only possibility." They hiked three kilometers to the edge of the village. Lucas stopped and pointed to a small white sign: FEURKOGEL written in faded red letters. He raised his hands in desperation. "Let's go to the train station. Jon, you buy our tickets in separate cars. Here's some money."

Jon nodded and walked into the station. Moments later he returned with the tickets. "I know a café near here, Zwei Konig, Two Kings."

Lucas said, "Lead the way."

They walked three blocks and entered the Zwei Konig, a small café with a cluster of grape twigs hanging above the door. Jon pointed and said, "That means the owner grows his own grapes." He smiled and gave a thumbs-up.

They went in separately. At the entry was a large glass case with various meats: ham hocks, blocks of bacon, pig's feet, and tongue. Another section was breakfast fare: scrambled eggs, fried sliced bacon, sausage, pumpernickel bread, muesli, and assorted grains. They watched as Jon selected items and paid at the cashier situated at the end of the case. After a short while, Lucas and Abel picked out their breakfast, and they sat alone at different tables.

Lucas sat at a secluded table next to a window, facing the door. As he tasted his eggs and sausage, a stranger wearing a black felt hat and topcoat sat down at Jon's table. Jon nervously glanced at Lucas as the stranger started to talk.

Another stranger stopped by Lucas's table. "Welcome to our village. May I join you?"

Lucas nodded and motioned to a chair.

The stranger said, "I have not seen you here before."

"First time."

"You're very young. Why are you not in the Wehrmacht?"

Lucas patted his left chest. "Bad heart."

"I'm sorry." The stranger straightened in his chair. "My name is Karl Unger. Yours?"

"Hans Koenig." They shook hands.

Unger looked at him as if he wanted to say something else. "Sorry to interrupt. I just wanted to greet you and welcome you." He left the café.

Later, they exited one at a time. When Lucas came out, he saw Abel across the street sitting on a bench under an elm tree. He crossed the road, walked past Abel, and continued down the dirt sidewalk. They met at a magazine stand three blocks away. Jon wasn't with Abel.

"Have you seen Jon? I wonder who he was talking to."

Abel looked down the street. "Here he comes. Seems in a hurry."

Short of breath, Jon walked to them. "Sorry I'm late; had to go to the WC."

"Who were you talking to in the café?" Lucas said, in an accusatory tone.

"Oh, that man has hired me for hikes and rappelling tours. I've known him a long time."

"Did you schedule a tour with him?"

"Not now. Maybe later in spring."

Lucas and Abel glanced at each other. Abel said, "Let's go to the train station; we leave in an hour."

Lucas stopped them on the way. "I'm worried about Nazi guards at Altaussee. We'll jump from the train before arrival. There's a bridge over the river. The tracks run close to the rail; jump over the rail. I'll pick the place. When they announce Altaussee as next station, get up and follow me to the space between the last two cars. We'll jump when the train slows for arrival."

Jon said, "I don't think that's necessary."

"It wasn't a suggestion, Jon. You jump when we jump. Understand?"

"Yes, of course."

They boarded the train bound for Altaussee. Lucas watched the forest glide by next to a swiftly moving stream. They began to climb as they approached the heart of Salzkammergut.

Thirty minutes later, a conductor walked through their car and called, "Next stop, Bad Ischl." Lucas removed his Beretta from his pants pocket and slid it under a magazine. As they pulled into the station, he saw armed Nazi guards pacing the platform.

The train pulled to a stop, and the guards came aboard. The three Bonzos sat silent and still. A guard entered their crowded car and randomly checked passenger papers, looking at the IDs of all young men. He stopped by Jon, who handed over his papers. They casually conversed as the guard noted every page of his packet. He yanked a sheet out of the folder. "What is this?

Jon said, "My hunting license; I am a hunter."

They laughed, and the guard moved on to Lucas. He looked at his ID, studied the photo, and memorized his face. "Are you having a nice trip, Major Koenig?"

Lucas answered. "Yes, but spring snow is not so good."

The train whistle sounded and the guard hurried from the car.

The train pulled away and went through Bad Goisern without stopping. Twenty minutes later the conductor yelled, "Altaussee." Lucas's heart quickened as he thought of his father and Erika. Where were they? Memories flooded his mind. He knew the countryside and remembered when the railroad was built.

Then he saw the stream that ran parallel to the tracks. He got up and walked toward the rear into the space between cars. He stood next to the door watching for the place where the stream came nearer the tracks. Minutes passed. Abel and Jon joined him. Suddenly, he saw railing. He kicked the doors open and leaped over the railing into water; Jon and Abel followed within seconds. They swam to the side away from the tracks and finally stood again on the sacred ground of Altaussee.

They walked into the forest and turned toward the village. Lucas figured they were not more than two miles from the church. After hiking through dense forest, they arrived. An armed guard stood at the main entrance. Lucas nodded to his right, and the three of them sneaked around the church to a service entrance.

Lucas tapped on the door. No answer. He turned the knob, and the door opened.

A dark-skinned man leaped from his chair. "Who are you?"

"Friends of Father Messmer." Lucas studied the stranger who limped as he turned to face them. His graying hair framed a narrow face and brown eyes that Lucas guessed had seen at least sixty years.

"Who are you?"

"I am Peter Hanl, the priest's assistant."

"Where is Otto?"

Peter looked at the floor for a moment and then turned back to Lucas. "Did you know Otto?"

Lucas nodded.

"He is no longer here, sir."

"Where is Father Messmer?"

"In his study."

Peter looked at their dirty wet clothes. "Wait here. I'll get the padre."

Abel said, "I wonder what happened to Otto."

"I don't know, but it worries me. I never heard Otto say anything against the Nazis."

"You think he was a spy? He had been here for years."

Father Messmer came out and his eyes widened. "Praise God, Lucas." They embraced and the priest stood back, his hands on Lucas's shoulders.

The priest saw Abel, went to him, and they hugged. "Are you okay, my son?"

Abel nodded.

Lucas asked, "Have you heard from Father?"

Father Messmer cleared his throat. "We have a lot to talk

about. Please come inside and we'll get you into dry clothes." He said to Pete, "Take them to our charity closet."

"Where is Erika, Father? Talk to me."

The padre pointed at Jon. "And who is this?"

"Our guide."

"I will talk to you, my son. Inside." The priest waved Lucas, Abel, and Jon to follow him. "Join me in the study after you have dried off and changed."

Later, when they entered the study, the priest asked Abel and Jon to give him some private time with Lucas. They walked out and closed the door.

Lucas sat down on a black leather couch and folded his hands. Father Messmer sat beside him and placed his hand on Lucas's knee.

"The Gestapo took me to headquarters and questioned me. I told them nothing." He placed his closed fist over his mouth. "I lied, Lucas. God forgive me."

"You did the right thing, Father—for mankind."

The priest frowned. "They are the personification of evil. They took Donner, my dog, away from me."

"Why? Did they hurt him?"

"They are going to train him as a war dog on the western front. They use German shepherds to smell out mines and explosives. He was my friend. They allowed me to return to the church, but I am forbidden to leave."

"Please tell me about my father."

The priest put his arm around Lucas and paused. "Edouard was arrested in his classroom."

"No . . ." Lucas stood, shaking. "Bastards."

"First he was interrogated by Kaltenbrunner. Rumor has it

that Kaltenbrunner questioned him about where you were and about a missing painting. Saints preserve us, the Nazis searched every building in the village: homes, churches, offices, and cafés. They tore down walls and dug up gardens. It was terrible."

"Father, is he alive?"

The priest squeezed both of Lucas's hands. "I don't know."

Lucas dropped to his knees and sobbed, shoulders shaking. Father Messmer rubbed his back. After he stopped crying, Lucas returned to the couch.

"Just tell me everything, please."

The priest took a deep breath. "After Kaltenbrunner's interrogation, Edouard was taken to Ebensee. They have a new director, Herr Bachmeier, I think, is his name. Resistance intelligence said that he personally questioned your father for days."

"Was he tortured?"

"Probably."

"Where is Erika?"

"She is confined at Villa Kerry. She's never alone, always with him or a female Gestapo agent."

"Does she look all right?"

"I have not seen her. I only know what I was told."

"Who told you this?"

"I do not know his name. He was from the Resistance."

Lucas got up and paced. "What's the condition of the Resistance?"

"Not good. Their leader is a coward communist; he doesn't know how to lead. They don't have enough men, arms, and ammunition. They are always short of money."

"What's the leader's name?"

"Victor Surgiyev."

"Do you know where I can find him?"

"He has headquarters in the forest." The padre slipped back in his chair and took a deep breath. "When would you like to see him?"

"Now."

"I must speak with the man who can take you there."

"When?"

"I will give you details in the morning. Good night."

23

In the forest high above Altaussee, Victor Surgiyev waited in his tent. It was absurd: a man of his stature should not wait. He paced and checked the entrance every few minutes. This Russian-born leader of the Austrian Resistance hated Nazis. During the Anschluss in 1938, Nazi soldiers stormed his modest home in the Vienna woods, gang-raped his wife, killed her and their infant son, and stabbed him in his left eye. A year later he returned to the site to find only a burned-out shell of black timbers, the cradle of his Nazi hatred. Victor relived that horror every day of his life, and many days he gained partial, empty revenge by killing Nazis. That's what he did. But his purpose in life had to be greater.

After the tragedy he joined the Maquis but was dishonorably discharged for disobeying orders and killing unarmed, defecting Wehrmacht soldiers and innocent German civilians. He then volunteered for the Austrian Resistance and took advantage of every opportunity to promote himself as an efficient, aggressive fighter who never hesitated to finish the kill. Victor took no prisoners. However, after reaching the upper echelons of command, he realized that he could order subordinates to do the killing while he lived in relative comfort.

Victor was short with a narrow face that drew attention to his eyes. The left eye was copper colored and stared straight ahead without moving. The green right eye moved as he talked. An inveterate cigarette smoker, he loved to wrap his yellow-stained fingers around a beer mug. He also enjoyed frequent liaisons with ladies.

Standing at the tent entrance, he saw Lucas and Abel approach, blindfolded. He stepped outside and ordered the blindfolds removed. "Well, the priest tells me our famous criminals have returned and want to have a word with me."

"We're not criminals," Lucas said as he looked around at dirty tents, scattered firearms, and scraggly fighters, smoking and sleeping.

Surgiyev waved toward the tent. "Come inside. We talk."

Sitting on a chair with a brown canvas seat, Lucas stared at a green ribbon above Victor's medals on his tunic. On it was written in blood red the initials O5. "What's the ribbon for?"

"It is the sign of the Austrian Resistance. The five stands for the letter *E*, the fifth letter of the alphabet, and the *O* is for the first letter of the abbreviation for Austria: *Österreich.* Only leaders of the Austrian Resistance wear it." He paused. "Enough about ribbons. This morning I received some worrisome intelligence. Last night armed Nazi troop carriers unloaded eight coffin-sized wooden crates into the salt mine. My informer, a villager, saw them and was alarmed by the size of the boxes."

"What time was this?"

"Midnight."

"We must find out what's in those crates." Lucas nodded at Abel, and they both stood.

"Where are you going? We must discuss how to proceed."

Lucas sat down and leaned forward, elbows on knees. He looked into Victor's eyes. "How is your operation going?"

"Not so good, my friend, but our Resistance in the north has had a great success. We recaptured the Castle Iter and killed hundreds of Bosch." Victor wiped his forehead with his sleeve. "We cannot have such a victory here. There is no castle, but we have great riches: the Nazi-confiscated art in the salt mine. We must protect it. We wait to see whether the Germans or Americans arrive first. We have few men. The villagers are cowards and will not join the fight. No one is interested in us until they need protection from the Bosch. We do have a few miners, but they have nothing to use in the fight. The main problem is we have no money. Arms dealers do not deal without money . . . a lot of money."

"Have you had many Wehrmacht defectors?"

"Oh yes, but they are tired of fighting and want to just sit on their asses and drink beer."

Lucas said, "I know you're doing the best you can, but without help, you have an impossible task—unless the Americans come soon."

"I know that," said Surgiyev, "but if the German army arrives first, what happens? Who gets the art?"

Lucas stood up, took a few steps toward the opening, and turned to Surgiyev. "No matter who gets here first, we have to be ready, or all will be lost."

The leader stood also. "So, you said 'we.' Are you interested in joining our forces?"

"Yes, along with my friend here, Abel Graf."

Victor nodded and scratched his chin. "I don't know. You are wanted men. I could call the Nazis and collect a big reward."

Lucas laughed. "Oh yes, I'm quite sure they would arrest me and pay you off. Then they would annihilate you, your men, and this dismal excuse for a Resistance. Let's not talk nonsense."

"What are you suggesting?"

"Besides men, arms, and money, the thing most lacking here is organization. The Resistance must be run as a well-financed military unit with efficiency, wisdom, and . . . leadership."

Surgiyev looked up at Lucas and clenched both fists. "No matter what plan you have, I must remain as leader. On that there can be no compromise."

"Of course," Lucas said. "We need you as the leader, but I can help you reach sources that you don't even know exist and obtain the things we need. I'm close to the miners and know a lot of villagers who would join us in the fight. It can't get much worse than it is now."

Victor scratched his face. "I'll think about it."

"There's no time to think. We must act. Now." Lucas turned toward Abel. "He is ready to join. We have been on the run, lucky to still be alive."

"Does Kaltenbrunner still have your lady in his house?"

"Yes."

"Will that interfere with your work in the Resistance?"

"Not now, but at some point I will free her. I'm glad you mentioned Kaltenbrunner. Because of the threat of the Nazis destroying the mine, it might be a good idea to ask Kaltenbrunner for permission to move the most important art pieces to a safer place in the mine: St. Barbara's Chapel."

"Do you really think that Nazi monster would help us?"

"It's possible. He will need help to survive after the war. We can offer that to him."

"Never. I only look forward to pissing on his grave. We must fight our way in. Now, would you please step outside so I can talk to my officers?"

As Lucas and Abel left, five men dressed in mixed green and tan uniforms walked into the tent and jerked the flap shut.

Lucas and Abel walked to the edge of the compound under the supervision of a guard, rifle at the ready.

"What do you think?" Abel asked.

"It's hard to know. He's a weakling who blames his failures on everyone else. We must make it work. This Resistance unit, as poor as it is, is the only platform we have to carry out our mission. If you could just—"

"Here he comes."

They walked back toward Victor, and he motioned them into the tent.

No one spoke for a few tense moments. Victor said, "My officers agree that your plan could help our situation. So, give me some details of what we should do. Notice that I said 'we.'"

Lucas raised both hands as in surrender. "'We' is the correct word, and you are the boss. The first thing is to contact the head of the miners and enlist their help. I can convince them to join us. I know the manager of the local gendarmerie and am sure he will give us weapons and ammunition. Regarding the Wehrmacht defectors, when they surrender, they will have to pay a handsome sum for us to accept them. If they don't have the money, they can steal it. They're good at that. Also, we can spread the word by radio to German troops that we are receptive to their defection, but that it will cost money. A good phrase at the end of the message could be 'how much is your life worth?'"

Victor smiled. "I thought of all those things but haven't had time to implement them."

Lucas winked at Abel. They all shook hands, and Lucas and Abel were transported to the village where they walked to their hideout in a concealed room in the church basement.

24

High atop a hill overlooking Altaussee, Kaltenbrunner sat by a raging fire in Villa Kerry, the home he had acquired after evicting the owners.

Contemplating his fate after the war, he realized that he needed more security than a few miners and villagers pledging to help him. He regretted the mass slaughter, not because of the death of innocent people, but because it would no doubt diminish the villagers' willingness to help him after the war.

After two hours of profound thought and a half bottle of Kummel Schnapps, he placed a telephone call to Uberlieutenant Greiner.

"Kurt, order an immediate assembly of my most trusted advisers. Do you remember their names?"

"I am not sure, sir. Please give me their names, and I will write them down."

A bit disgruntled at his assistant's forgetfulness, Kaltenbrunner slowly pronounced them, "Wilfred Werner, director of the local Gestapo unit and his assistant Erich Kroger; and Georg Becker, Eigruber's assistant. And Kurt, you should be here as well."

Two hours later the advisers joined Kaltenbrunner in his

library. Greiner had not yet arrived. After champagne and idle chatter, they began the discussion of their survival after the war.

All three Nazis proposed different scenarios with one common theme: kill as many Austrians, Americans, and Jews as possible before they escaped. Despite their pompous hubristic babble, each of their plans had a common flaw that begged one question: how can we escape?

Greiner burst into the room. "I am sorry to be late, mein Commandant."

Kaltenbrunner scowled and said in an irritated voice, "Take a seat, Greiner."

"Sir, I was delayed by an incredible telephone call. May I have permission to speak?"

Kaltenbrunner nodded.

Greiner straightened his coat and strolled to the center of the room. "I have it on the highest authority that the *Mona Lisa* is for sale."

The advisors gasped and chatted among themselves.

Kaltenbrunner interrupted, "Please, gentlemen. Continue, Karl."

Greiner, enjoying his sudden celebrity, said, "Goering's art expert, Eric Kanner, who handles all the purchases of Goering's masterpieces, telephoned me with this startling information. He discovered the *Mona Lisa* in an underworld Russian market and has been ordered by Goering to buy it for one million Deutsche marks. But Kanner, always looking to make money for himself, said that for certain considerations, he could make it available to you." He paused. "Sir, Kanner said that the *Mona Lisa* will never sell for the pittance of one million marks and suggested doubling the price."

All of the senior Nazis were thrilled at the expectation of such a major coup.

Kaltenbrunner called for order. "There could be no better bargaining chip than the *Mona Lisa* to assure our safety after the war." His mind immediately began to churn out devious schemes he could use to save himself. He would get the money and throw his advisers to the dogs.

Werner said, "Here is an idea. We can enhance our advantage by gifting the *Mona Lisa* to the Americans, who in turn will give it to the French, and we will be free and rich. Glorious."

Another said, "Yes, imagine the celebration at the Louvre and de Gaulle's indebtedness to Eisenhower, while we are basking in the sun in Argentina."

Listening to the chatter, Kaltenbrunner thought, you all are stupid. I will sell it to the highest bidder and keep all the profit.

He said, "Never fear. I will take care of all of you." He raised his glass. "Gentlemen, I propose a toast to acquiring the *Mona Lisa*. She is the key not only to our surviving but also to our flourishing in wealth." He turned to Karl Greiner. "Tell Kanner that I will pay two million Deutsche marks. Arrange delivery of the painting to my cellar here at Villa Kerry." He paused. "I may have to dig up some of the gold in my garden."

25

The next morning Lucas and Abel sat at a table set with scrambled eggs, Semmeln (breakfast bread), marmalade, sliced ham, and steaming black coffee.

Spreading marmalade and butter on the Semmeln, Victor looked at Lucas and said, " Do you have a plan?"

"Yes, and it includes you and your men. But first I would like to hear your thoughts on this operation."

Victor stood and began to pace. "Let me call my officers in to discuss this." He sent his aide to gather them.

With his officers present, Victor described the situation. "Are there any comments?"

The second in command snapped to attention. "Thank you, mein Commandant, for the privilege of giving my opinion. Most importantly, we have to be prepared for an ambush when we go to the mine. This attack must be a total annihilation. The Nazi guards rotate shifts at the mine entrance. Their sleeping quarters are on the ground floor of the administration building. We should coordinate simultaneous surprise attacks on their quarters while they are sleeping as well as the mine entrance. This total kill will prevent any backup support at the mine."

Victor stood up. "Well said, Karl. How did you learn these things about their quarters?"

"I have a friend in the kitchens. Olga. She hates the Bosch; they killed her father on the eastern front. We are . . . how do you say . . . close."

The other officers applauded.

"This attack will be succesful." Victor rubbed his chin. "Perhaps your friend Olga in the kitchen could arrange to deliver hot coffee, laced with cyanide, to the guards at the main entrance just before we launch."

Karl asked, "Do we have a supply of cyanide?"

"Yes. It is locked in a case in the storage cabinet. I have the only key." Victor surveyed the group and stared at Lucas. "So, are we all in agreement?"

Lucas rose. "I think we have the beginning of a successful plan; it must, however, be staged: first, attack the mine and gain control; second, move art to St. Barbara's Chapel; third, blow up the mine entrance. Then we must protect the entrance."

"Of course," shouted Victor. "We will place guards there."

The tent was silent; all, including Victor, were impressed by the plan.

Victor glanced at Lucas who nodded with a smile. "Thank you, Karl. Would anyone else like to speak?"

Another officer stood, raised his fist, and cried out, "We must kill as many Bosch as possible."

All yelled and applauded, except Lucas.

Victor stared at Lucas. "What do you think?"

"It will take a few days to organize the miners, get arms from the gendarmarie, and arrange trucks for transportation. We must remember that the bombs and art are the critical targets, not slaughtering Nazis."

Victor took charge. "It's a relatively simple operation. We will deploy snipers at strategic points. If there are guards still alive after their coffee, we will wait for your signal to fire. Simply raise your right arm, and we will kill the rest of the guards."

"Tell your snipers to be patient."

"Who will be with you?"

"My partner Abel Graf and three miners who have offered to help move the bombs out of the mine and the art into St. Barbara's Chapel. It's the safest place in the mine." He paused. "I'm a little concerned about one of the miners. He's a fanatic Nazi hater and short-tempered, but strong as a bull."

"I like him," Victor said as he stood and clapped his hands once. "Let me know when you are ready. I'll bring my best snipers—they don't miss."

26

Three Days Later

Moonlight shone through naked birch limbs creating dancing shadows on the stone walkway to the mine entrance. The breeze scraped bare limbs together: a staccato death cadence fracturing the coffinlike silence, a prelude to the impending slaughter.

Dressed as miners, Lucas, Abel, and three men who worked there every day walked toward the entrance. One of them was the quick-tempered miner who hated Nazis. Lucas felt the same thundering hammer in his chest as when he trudged up the hill on his first trip to the mine.

Through the darkness, Lucas saw three guards, their limp arms slumped over a parapet near the mine entrance. On the nearby wall sat a tin coffee carafe, steam floating from its spout.

Numerous explosions erupted from the administration building, decimating the ground floor. A screaming Nazi guard, his clothes afire, bolted through a hole in the wall. The short-tempered miner shouted, "Du bastard," and shot the burning Nazi in the chest. He dropped like a stone.

In the same instant Lucas raised his right arm. "Down." Rifle fire crackled from the forest.

A platoon of Wehrmacht soldiers charged from the mine

and were quickly slaughtered by machine-gun fire from Victor's Resistance fighters. They joined Lucas's group and dragged bodies, intestines, severed arms and legs, brains, and shards of skull behind rocks. Four Resistance fighters stood guard at the mine entrance.

The miners drove the entire entourage on Hunde to St. Barbara's Chapel. From there they rocketed down the wooden slides and finally reached the Mineral Cabinet.

Only one large wooden crate lay in the chamber. A miner ripped off the cover, and Lucas swiped away the covering straw. Inside he saw a five-hundred-kilogram airplane bomb that was stenciled on its side in black block letters: USAF. No detonator was attached.

Lucas said, "Victor, take your men to search for the other bombs. There are seven more." He turned to the miners and Abel. "Let's move this art to St. Barbara's Chapel." He risked a glimpse at the vertical crevice where he'd hidden the *Mona Lisa*; the small sentinel rock was in the exact position he had left it in. He breathed a sigh of relief.

Over the next several hours, Lucas directed the miners, and several of Victor's soldiers did the heavy lifting and transported some fifty paintings and statues, including Van Eyck's *Ghent Altarpiece*, Michelangelo's *Bruges Madonna*, and Canaletto's *Venice: The Doge's Palace and the Riva degli Schiavoni*, to St. Barbara's Chapel.

After the art had been moved, they returned to the Mineral Cabinet just as a joyous Victor returned. "We found the other seven bombs, and they are being moved out of the mine and placed just outside the entrance under the birch trees. It will take several hours."

"Good work."

Lucas then turned to Abel. "Where is the nearest radio station?"

"Bad Aussee. What are you thinking?"

"There will be chaos outside. Maybe we can add to the confusion. Come with me."

Walking through the mine entrance, they met the village mayor and a gaggle of curiosity seekers.

"Where are the guards?" asked the mayor.

Lucas smiled. "We heard that they have defected."

The crowd murmured among themselves and ran off to spread the news.

Lucas and Abel drove to nearby Bad Aussee and located the small two-story building housing the radio station. Abel quickly set about adjusting the radio equipment. After five minutes he handed the microphone to Lucas. "Click the button and speak to our countrymen."

With no hesitation, Lucas clicked the button. "This is Radio Free Austria, dedicated to regaining Austria's freedom. This morning, Austrian Resistance fighters killed the adjutant of the guards and all Nazi soldiers guarding the mine entrance. The remainder of the Nazi garrison died in explosions in the administration building. We know that the Resistance entered the mine, but we have no further information. The people of Austria have the right to know that for years Nazi thieves have been storing a hoard of masterworks of famous painters in the mine. Radio Free Austria has learned that our nearby forests are filled with our brave Resistance heroes who are chasing the German Sixth Army in an effort to capture its leader, General Seidl. Many Nazi soldiers have defected. Beware of any strangers who come to your door.

High-ranking Nazis have migrated to hide in Altaussee. They call it their redoubt. Beware of all German soldiers, but if they try to surrender, accept them."

Abel switched on the Austrian national anthem, "Land der Berge, Land am Strome" (Land of Mountains, Land of Streams).

Lucas fought back tears. "Have faith, my countrymen. Austria will soon be free."

As the anthem ended, Abel switched off the power.

Lucas slapped his shoulder and laughed. "Let's go to Victor's headquarters."

Victor greeted Lucas and Abel in his tent. "I missed your broadcast, but the villagers are happy, singing and playing music in the streets." Victor motioned to chairs, and they all sat down. "While you were on the air, we captured General Seidl. He is our prisoner, along with twenty of his henchmen. The trial is about to start. We're holding him in the forest. Come with me."

They approached a clearing in the forest where two groups of ten Nazi soldiers stood bound in a circle. A single soldier, stripped of his ribbons, stood tied to a tree some twenty meters from the clearing.

One of Victor's leaders called the trial to order and read the charges; if found guilty, General Seidl would be executed. There were no attorneys. Victor's troops were the jury. At the completion of the reading of the charges, they shouted, "Guilty." The twenty soldiers were told to line up, and a firing squad got into position. General Seidl stood alone, tied to a tree.

Victor said to Seidl, "You will be the last to die. You must watch your henchmen's slaughter."

A veil of silence fell over the court.

Lucas stepped next to Victor and whispered, "Why don't you

give them a choice? Suspend their sentence if they agree to join us in our fight. They must surrender all their weapons and give us all of their money."

Victor said, "I thought of that but fear that would upset my men. They want blood."

"Divide all the money among your men. That will change their thinking."

Victor turned to his troops. "Stand at ease." He approached General Seidl. "We have decided to give you a chance."

Seidl, defiantly arrogant, stared at him. "And what is this chance?"

"Join us in our fight against your former comrades. They are doomed. After the war we will acknowledge to the American command that you helped us. It could save your life."

Seidl thought for a moment and said, "Agreed. Let me inform my men."

Victor turned to his troops. "Release the prisoners."

The stunned resistance fighters followed orders and rushed to Victor's side for an explanation.

"Brilliant idea," Victor said to no one in particular. "We have gained power."

27

Fearing the American troops would not arrive before Eigruber destroyed the art, Lucas initiated his plan. He ordered that dynamite charges be placed around the entrance.

Lucas stood with Victor behind a large boulder one hundred meters away. He placed his hand on the chief explosives engineer's shoulders. "I hope this works."

"It will, Herr Brunn. It must."

A miner threw the detonator switch and six tons of explosives with three hundred detonators ignited an ear-splitting explosion. A gigantic rockslide speckled with shining red rock salt closed the entrance, belching debris and a white cloud of smoke into the adjacent forest.

Lucas sighed. "No matter what happens now, the treasure trove of stolen art is safe inside the mountain."

Victor arrived as the dust settled. He said to Lucas, "Do you know Herr Teuber?

"Yes. He's Erika's father. Why?"

"He wants to speak with you."

Lucas turned and ran down the trail to the road where Abel waited on his motorcycle. Hopeful that Erika had returned, they rushed to the Teuber home.

Klaus invited Lucas and Abel into the parlor, but Abel remained outside. Klaus said to Lucas, "Would you like some tea?"

"No thanks. Have you heard from Erika?"

"No. I wish she was here with us. I have information about your father."

Lucas clutched the padded arm of his chair and leaned forward.

Klaus laced his fingers, pressed his lips into a thin line, and paused before saying, "Edouard was executed and cremated at Ebensee."

Lucas screamed and fell forward on his knees, his head buried in his forearms. "No. My God. When did you hear this?"

"Early this morning."

"Who told you?"

"A Resistance fighter. I can't give you his name."

"Was he certain?"

"Yes, I'm afraid so."

"Where are his ashes?"

Klaus turned up his palms and thought for a moment. "His ashes sail in the sun, ride on the rain, and soar to mountaintops, where only eagles soar."

Lucas bowed his head and then looked at Erika's father. "That's beautiful. Thank you. Where did you learn those words?"

"They come from God."

Neither spoke for several moments.

"I knew this would happen. The Nazi bastards will pay."

Lucas ran from the Teuber home, Klaus calling after him.

"What's wrong?" Abel said.

"The Nazis murdered my father and burned him in the ovens."

"Lucas, I'm so sorry."

"Take me to my to mother's gravesite."

"Get in."

Lucas climbed into the sidecar and didn't speak until they reached the path leading to her grave.

Lucas hopped from the sidecar. "Wait here."

Abel moved to follow him.

"Please, Abel. I must go alone."

Lucas ran to his mother's headstone, moved the small stones, dug up the package, and ripped it open. He threw the damp outer envelope aside, and held three pages filled with chemistry formulas and equations. One equation was underlined with an arrow pointing to his father's sketch of an airplane wing's attachment to the fuselage. He folded the papers and slipped them into his jacket pocket.

He ran to Abel. "Please take me to the church."

28

Lucas rushed into Father Messmer's office and said, "Father, do you remember the night that I left?"

"Vividly, Lucas. All of the heart-wrenching fear. I was wrong to discourage you from leaving."

"You were only trying to protect me. Do you remember the package that my father gave me?"

"Yes. What did you do with it?"

"I buried it by my mother's grave. Today Klaus Teuber told me that the Nazis executed my father. I raced to her gravesite and retrieved it." Lucas removed the pages from the envelope and handed them to the priest. "Tell me what you think."

Father Messmer wiped away tears, sat down at his desk, put on his glasses, adjusted the desk lamp, and began to read. After several moments he looked at Lucas. "I don't understand the equations, but this obviously is the formula for a powerful glue for use in building airplanes."

"It's more than that, Father. The Nazis have had problems with their fighters and even bombers with their wings falling off in flight. When I was with the Maquis in Ardennes, I actually saw a Messerschmitt fall from the sky with only one wing attached. If the Nazis got their hands on this, it could change the outcome of the war. Now I understand what Father meant when he said this letter could save thousands of lives."

The priest rose from his chair and handed the papers back to Lucas. "What are you going to do with this information?"

"I'll show this to the Americans when they arrive and ask for their advice."

"You must be cautious and claim ownership of this document. It could be worth a fortune."

Lucas said, "I'm not interested in making money from Father's work."

"Perhaps not, but just remember what I said. Now you must get some rest. I hid a mattress, blankets, and pillows in the cellar. Come, I'll show you."

29

The next morning Lucas, Abel, and Victor drove to the mine. Austrian Resistance guards stood at the entrance welcoming advance platoons of Patton's Third Army.

A captain stepped forward and extended his hand to Lucas. "Mr. Brunn, I'm Captain Robert Treadway, US Third Army. Your colleagues told me about your heroics. It's an honor to meet you."

"Thank you. I'm happy you're here, Captain."

"Well, it's been uneventful so far. American soldiers rode in a Jeep through the village and claimed capture as they raised the American flag atop the bell tower. No shots were fired." He nodded toward the huge pile of stone blocking the mine entrance. "Looks like we have a lot of work ahead. My men will make short work of that."

Lucas said, "No one knows what lies behind the rubble. It could take days to remove it."

"We'll have it cleared by 1600 hours." Captain Treadway turned to his corporal and said, "Get it done." The corporal saluted and trotted toward other American troops.

At 1630 hours that afternoon, Lucas, Abel, and Victor escorted the captain and corporal into the mine.

Captain Treadway, who spoke with a deep southern accent,

introduced his corporal. "Mr. Brunn, shake hands with Corporal Morris Johns, the pride of Tupelo, Mississippi. We're in charge of protecting and caring for fine arts and monuments. We're the Monuments Men."

Near the altar in St. Barbara's Chapel, where Lucas delivered his first prayer, he stood next to the *Ghent Altarpiece*. Arms extended, palms up, he said, "Take them home." Lucas realized he would eventually have to return the *Mona Lisa* to authorities, but he decided to wait, just in case.

On leaving the mine, Captain Treadway said, "Good job, Mr. Brunn. We'll take full responsibility for the art now."

Lucas said, "Sir, I have some papers I'd like for you to evaluate." Treadway studied the three pages and shrugged his shoulders. "No idea what this means. Come with me and I'll show you to our JAG officer."

The legal officer called in a chemical engineer, and they reviewed Edouard's thesis.

The engineer said, "The title of your father's thesis is 'Relative Metal Bonding Capacities of Epoxy and Cyanoacrylate Glues in Aeronautics.' He simply combined these two glues and heated them to 350 degrees Fahrenheit. This produced a product with extraordinary metal bonding capacities. His note on the last page reads: 'Reliable product to prevent military aircraft wing separation.'" He paused. "We'd like your permission to turn this over to US Air Force officials, including attorneys, to have it copyrighted in your name. This could well be critical to the outcome of the war, and, as the owner of this document, you may become very wealthy."

30

One week later at Resistance tent headquarters, Lucas, Abel, Victor, and officers of the American Third Army, the Austrian Resistance, and a few villagers were involved in heated discussions about hunting down Kaltenbrunner. He had supposedly been sighted in Strobl, where his wife and two daughters lived. On Kaltenbrunner's trail, Lucas and Victor had captured six high-ranking Nazis, all headed to their alpine retreat to make their last stand. Other rumors of sightings of the Nazi monster abounded, all without substance.

A young lad, looking at the floor and twisting his fingers, came forward.

Lucas rushed to him. "Do you know what we're talking about?"

The lad looked up into Lucas's eyes and in a soft voice said, "*Ja.*"

"*Was gibt?*"

The boy spoke hesitantly, slowly pronouncing each word, seemingly aware of the importance of what he had to say. "Herr Kaltenbrunner paid my brother to be his guide."

"Do you know where they went?"

The lad kept his eyes on the floor, frequently glancing at the entrance. He said nothing for a few minutes, then replied, "I am not sure. I heard them talking about the hunters' hut in Wildensee Alm. There were three German soldiers. One was a tall German who had some maps."

"Has your brother returned?"

"No. I worry."

Lucas asked a lady villager to take care of the boy, and she led him away.

Lucas cleared the room except for Abel, Victor as Chief of Austrian Resistance, and US Army Captain Robert Treadway, with nine platoon members.

Lucas looked at Abel. "Do you know the area?"

"Yes. The Wildensee Alm is an alpine pasture high above the timberline on the Loser plateau. Spring snow two meters deep is usual. It requires a rugged five-hour hike through dense forest and open pasture dotted with huge rocks to reach the hut."

Lucas spoke to Captain Treadway. "Will you help us?"

"Yes. I've already obtained clearance for the mission."

"How should we do it?'

"We have the advantage of you and your friend Abel knowing the terrain. We should plan a midnight departure." He glanced at his watch. "That would give us an 0500 arrival time. If Kaltenbrunner is in the hut, he'll have plenty of armed help. Best to surprise them at sunrise."

"Agreed," said Abel. "The hut sits exposed on a bare ridge on the downslope of the crest of the Loser plateau, so there's no place to hide. We need the element of surprise as an ally."

At 2200 hours, on May 6, 1945, the group planned final strategies for the mission. Captain Treadway would lead the mission with his platoon armed with rifles, pistols, ammunition, hand grenades, and two bazookas. The final plan specified that one man would approach the hut. If someone opened the door, he would ask for directions to Techlos, a small village on the opposite side of the Loser. Lucas volunteered. Dressed in native Austrian hiking gear, he wore spiked shoes for the icy terrain. "If someone answers my knock, he will not be Kaltenbrunner. I'll ask for directions, but what if he gives the directions and closes the door?'

Captain Treadway nodded. "By that time we will have arrived at the opposite side of the hut, out of sight from the porch. If he tries to close the door, kick it open, and we'll storm in." He paused. "Here, slip this small Beretta into your pocket. But remember, we want to take Kaltenbrunner alive."

Lucas looked at the Beretta and thought of Erika. He wondered if he could kill again—if he could resist shooting the Nazi beast.

At 2400 hours, they walked through the village, along the lake, into dense forest, and above the timberline, encountering snow and bitter cold winds. One of the platoon corporals slipped and fell off the trail, breaking his left leg. A fellow platoon soldier helped him back to Altaussee. At dawn, after a five-hour trek, they reached a snow-covered pass, and using high-powered field glasses, they could see the hut three hundred meters in the distance. Winds blasted snow into tornadolike funnels that resembled dancing commas on a floor of white death.

Lucas turned to Captain Treadway, who stood next to his second in command. "I would like to request permission to go in first."

"I planned to go with three of my men."

"A group would be easier to spot. They'll just think I'm a local villager."

Treadway rubbed his hands together and looked at his second in command, who smiled and nodded.

———

At 0500 Lucas began his approach to the hut from its blind west side. He froze at the chirp of a bird to his right. He held his breath. Was it a signal? He studied the surrounding terrain. He smiled to himself and thought that the bird must be as cold as he was.

He neared the hut, leaned against the faded, peeling, dirty gray paint, looked back, and saw the rest of the mission members slowly advancing. No lights were on, no smoke came from the chimney, the wood shutters were closed, and no recent foot tracks were visible in the snow. He stepped onto the porch and knocked. No answer. Another knock, and after an eternity, a man dressed in heavy hunter's gear opened the door and stared over Lucas's shoulder. He nodded and Lucas followed him into the hut.

The main room was cold, the stove now a refrigerator. Three men entered from the back room. The man who answered the door introduced two hunters and a tall man with a pince-nez and black hair. He wore an Austrian green coat and trousers. He reached to shake Lucas's hand, but Lucas backed away. Captain Treadway and Abel burst into the room, rifles at the ready. The platoon jumped onto the porch, waiting.

The tall man ignored them and smiled at Lucas. "My name is Dr. Josef Unterwogen. I am on my way to help an injured skier in Techlos."

Lucas stared at the disfiguring scar running from the doctor's left ear to the corner of his mouth. A wave of nausea struck Lucas as a kaleidoscope of images of this animal making love to his beloved Erika went through his mind. He leaped forward and knocked Dr. Unterwogen to the floor, jumped astride his chest, and rammed his Beretta into Kaltenbrunner's mouth.

The Nazi sneered at Lucas. "My name is Dr. Josef Unterwogen."

"You Nazi bastard. You deserve a slow tortured death."

Captain Treadway pulled Lucas off and handcuffed Kaltenbrunner. Abel handcuffed the other three men.

Treadway asked, "Where is your guide?"

"He left after we arrived safely."

Captain Treadway said, "That's enough, Lucas. Let's move out."

Dr. Unterwogen said, "You are all confused. I realize that I resemble Herr Kaltenbrunner; it has caused many problems. My papers are in my coat pocket, just have a look at them."

"Where is Erika?"

"I'm afraid I don't know anyone by that name."

Lucas spat onto the Nazi's face and smashed his fist onto the scar. Again, the soldiers pulled him away.

Lucas stepped back, straightened his jacket, and stared at the scar. "When you step onto the gallows, be brave and decline the hood so that when the rope rips your head off, you can stare at the eternal fires of hell."

Captain Treadway said, "Come on. We can make the village by nightfall." He motioned to two corporals. "You two walk on each side of this 'doctor.' Keep his handcuffs on and loop a rope around his waist and keep it taut. Keep out of reach. If he makes a move, shoot him."

Lucas, Abel, Captain Treadway, the platoon, and their prisoners retraced their route down the trail. Kaltenbrunner continually voiced his innocence, claiming to be a local doctor on a mission of mercy.

Farmers just outside of the village saw the approaching group and followed. By the time Lucas, Treadway, and their prized prisoner reached the village, the crowd recognized Kaltenbrunner, and a large jeering mob walked alongside, shouting profanities. They reached the town square, now lighted by yellow streetlamps, and several raucous miners lunged toward the Nazi monster and had to be restrained by the military. The plan was to hold Kaltenbrunner under guard in the village jail until morning.

As the group stopped near the bell tower, a woman dressed in black, her face shadowed by a gray shawl, stepped before Father Messmer and handed him a folded note. She darted from the crowd, ran to Kaltenbrunner, hugged him, and buried her face on his chest. "Ernst, are you all right?"

Kaltenbrunner pushed her away. "I do not know this woman."

Treadway's sergeant guided the lady in black to his commander.

"Who are you?" Captain Treadway shouted.

Tears flowing down her cheeks, she looked at the ground and whispered, "I am his wife."

"Take her into custody." The aide led her away.

31

On May 10, 1945, at 0800 hours, Kaltenbrunner was moved under heavy guard to the Seevilla Hotel where a makeshift court had been assembled. US Third Army JAG Major Jarvis Thompson called to order the pre-indictment interrogation of Obergruppen-führer Ernst Kaltenbrunner. He slammed his gavel on the desk. "Gentlemen, it seems right and proper that we hold this hearing in the former Nazi headquarters. The American Third Army now controls Austria."

Those attending stood and applauded.

Major Thompson began reading the articles of indictment for crimes against humanity: "Ernst Kaltenbrunner, under the US Third Army's war crimes jurisdiction, you are charged with the following crimes."

Kaltenbrunner stared at those in attendance: US Third Army officers and two invited guests, Lucas Brunn and Abel Graf.

"One, committing and orchestrating crimes against humanity in Nazi concentration camps, including but not limited to Dachau, Matthausen, Ebensee, Buchenwald, Flossenburg, Nordhausen, and Auschwitz.

"Two, ordering inhumane treatment and execution of American airmen and other prisoners of war."

Kaltenbrunner jumped up and interrupted. "My name is Dr.

Josef Unterwogen. I am a private doctor captured on my way to aid an injured skier. I know nothing of the things you speak."

Major Thompson replied, "Obergruppenführer Ernst Kaltenbrunner, you do not have the right to address this hearing other than through your assigned counsel. Any further interruption by you will result in cessation of these hearings, and you will be immediately transferred for further processing at US Third Army headquarters in Munich."

Kaltenbrunner leaned to the side and whispered to his assigned defense attorney, JAG officer Captain Thomas Brunson.

Brunson rose. "Major Thompson, may it please the court, my client wishes to make a statement."

A tomblike silence settled over the court.

Major Thompson said, "Captain Brunson, you may escort your client to the bench, accompanied by prosecuting attorneys."

Kaltenbrunner, hands cuffed behind, followed his attorney and the prosecution to the bench.

Major Thompson spoke to Captain Brunson. "Do you know the contents of the statement your client wishes to make?"

"I do not, sir."

Thompson drew his lips into a fine line and glared at the prisoner. "Make your statement. You have three minutes."

Kaltenbrunner squared his shoulders. "It is time stop this foolishness. I do not recognize your authority to judge me. I confess that I am indeed Obergruppenführer Ernst Kaltenbrunner, chief of the Austrian SS. I am innocent of all charges, had nothing to do with our special camps, and, since the Anschluss, have only tried to help the Austrian people. Throughout my military career, I only followed the orders of my Führer, Adolf Hitler. All of that aside, I have an astounding announcement. I wish to inform this court that I have possession of Leonardo da Vinci's *Mona Lisa*."

Members of the court gasped and began to mumble.

Major Thompson rapped his gavel. "Order. Quiet." He turned to Kaltenbrunner. "Have you finished your statement?"

"No. I have an offer for the US Army, the Allies, and France. Dismiss all charges against me, and I will give you the *Mona Lisa*. General Eisenhower may then return it to the French, becoming a world hero. And I make this offer without any payment demands."

His words stunned the court.

Major Thompson's face reddened. "You Nazi . . ." The major composed himself. "How dare you insult this court with your sleazy attempt to buy your freedom! Return to your seat!"

Lucas stood and raised his hand.

Major Thompson recognized him from a previous introduction. "Yes, Mr. Brunn."

"May I speak in private to you and other officers of the court?"

"The court is recessed. Return the prisoner to his cell. Mr. Brunn and officers of the court, join me in my chambers."

They sat around a conference table, and Major Thompson invited Lucas to speak.

"I know that Kaltenbrunner's *Mona Lisa* is fake."

"And how do you know that?"

"On Christmas Eve, 1944, on a mission for the Austrian Resistance, I stole into the salt mine to find out what was in the large crates delivered to the mine by Nazi convoys. I found a huge cache of stolen art, including *The Adoration of the Mystic Lamb* and others. I was stunned to also discover the *Mona Lisa*, hidden under scraps of lumber and rock salt. I identified the painting and replaced it in the case. I couldn't just leave her there, so I hid the case in a small crevice in the Mineral Cabinet and covered the painting with rock salt and lumber scraps."

Major Thompson said, "Are you telling the truth?"

"I swear, sir. On my way out of the mine, I was confronted by a Wehrmacht guard whom I recognized as a former college classmate. He knocked me down and started to strangle me. I stabbed him in self-defense and left him. I don't know if he survived. My friend Abel Graf helped me escape to Graz in a stolen biplane. On landing we were attacked by Messerschmitts, and I suffered severe burns. After I recuperated, Abel Graf and I went to a meeting of the Austrian Resistance, where we were arrested and sentenced to death. The Nazis gave us a choice: join the Luftwaffe or face a firing squad. Abel and I joined, but defected by escaping from a Nazi airfield in Belgium. We joined the Maquis d'Ardennnes and later were turned over to American forces in Dinan."

Major Thompson threw up his hands. "This sounds like the movie script of a wartime thriller."

"It's all true, sir. The British SOE found out about our defection and flew us to London. We agreed to train as covert agents for an official mission: Operation Ebensburg. We parachuted into the Salzkammergut and made our way to Altaussee. Our mission: confirm that Nazi-looted art was stored in the salt mine and capture or kill Kaltenbrunner. On my return to Altaussee, I joined Victor Surgiyev and his Austrian Resistance fighters."

"Get to the point, Brunn. Tell me more about the *Mona Lisa*."

"I can lead you to her in the mine, sir."

"We will arrange that—and also procure Kaltenbrunner's *Mona Lisa* and have both examined by art experts."

A contingent of US Third Army officers, including members of the Monuments Men, followed Lucas into the mine and along the path he'd first taken on that daunting Christmas Eve. As they entered the Mineral Cabinet, they formed a large circle around Lucas. He walked to the shadowed crevice and removed his sentinel rock. He silently prayed that the *Mona Lisa* was there. He reached inside, but felt nothing. His heart pounded. A lieutenant handed him a flashlight. He caught a glimpse of white canvas.

"She's here," shouted Lucas. The lieutenant assisted as he removed the lumber and rock salt and slowly extracted the *Mona Lisa*.

Major Thompson said to Lucas, "Are you sure that's the same package you hid?"

"I am, sir."

Thompson turned and nodded to the Monuments Men. "Please return this item to the court. When we have received the other *Mona Lisa*, they will both be opened and inspected by an art expert."

32

Major Thompson reconvened the court at 1500 hours. Present were officers of the court and two invited guests, Lucas and Abel. Two armed guards stood on either side of Kaltenbrunner, who was handcuffed to his chair. Two paintings covered with purple velvet cloths stood on easels before the court.

Major Thompson slammed his gavel. "With the help of an Austrian patriot, the court has acquired what we believe to be the original *Mona Lisa*. The defendant, Ernst Kaltenbrunner, claims to own the *Mona Lisa*. The court has appointed Herr Karl Maier to examine both paintings. He is an art expert and restorer at the Bavarian National Museum in Munich. Herr Maier, please proceed."

Maier rose and walked to the picture removed from the basement of Villa Kerry. A guard removed the royal-purple cover, and the court gasped at the beauty of *La Joconde*. He walked before and around the painting, leaning close; using a magnification lens, he studied the lady's face, arms, and hands. For a moment, he stared at the greenish-brown eyes. He moved his head from side to side, paused, and frowned. He removed the back of the painting and examined the support structure for the pine-wood panel on which this painting had been rendered. After several minutes, he replaced the back of the painting.

The art restorer, clearly enjoying his moment of fame, waved for the cover of the second painting to be removed. Maier's eyes widened and he caught his breath. He moved with deliberate steps and repeated his previous examination. He leaned close and studied her hands and eyes—particularly her eyes. The back cover was replaced. He nodded his head from side to side, paused, and smiled. Entranced, he bowed, then raised his eyes and stared at the court.

Karl Maier's eyes moistened; he hugged himself and swayed, a soft tremor in his arms. He suddenly stepped back and nodded for the guard to cover the painting.

Major Thompson said, "Have you reached a conclusion, Herr Maier?"

The art expert's voice cracked when he tried to speak, and he coughed and tried to gather himself.

The court waited.

"I'd like to thank the court for this honor. Yes, I've made my conclusion."

A hush settled over the courtroom.

"The painting presented by Herr Kaltenbrunner is a copy."

Kaltenbrunner screamed and tried to stand. "How dare you, Jew bastard!"

The guards restrained the prisoner and forced him back into his chair.

Major Thompson stood and stared at the prisoner. "If you disrupt this court again, you will be remanded to your cell. Do you understand that?"

The Nazi monster bowed and nodded.

Maier continued, "As I was saying, the first painting is a rather good copy to be sure, but there is no doubt in my mind that it is a fake."

Major Thompson said, "Would you please give specifics of the criteria that you evaluated?"

"Of course. The *Mona Lisa*'s hands are very important. Da Vinci painted the right hand folded gently over the left, and did not show a wedding ring. The beauty of her hands proclaims her virtuosity. The forger of the other painting tried to copy her hands but couldn't. They appear stiff and the fingers are slightly apart. He must have intended it as a joke, as she has a pale circle around her left fourth finger, indicating that she had previously worn a wedding ring. I must say, that is indeed a sacrilege. In the first painting, her eyes are a shade of brown. In the second one—they are da Vinci's brown.

"In the second painting, the woman sits with her arms folded, which is a sign of her reserved posture. Her gaze is fixed on the observers and seems to follow them, perhaps welcoming a silent communication with admirers. Leonardo focused on the corners of her eyes and mouth. Even the youngest student of art knows that the true *Mona Lisa* has no eyelashes or eyebrows. In the forged copy, they are quite evident.

"And perhaps the most telling evidence is from inside the painting. First, the true *Mona Lisa* was painted on a poplar panel; the fake portrait was painted on a pine panel. In addition, several hundred years ago, the *Mona Lisa*'s poplar panel developed a small crack across her face. Restorers of that era placed an additional horizontal brace that, over the years, closed the crack. The fake portrait has no extra horizontal brace.

"I could go on for hours; suffice it to say that the painting recovered from the salt mine is the true *Mona Lisa*."

Major Thompson said, "Thank you for your service, Herr Maier. This court is adjourned. Return the defendant to his cell pending transfer to Munich and subsequently to the site of the final indictment and trial." He struck the gavel down one final time. Kaltenbrunner flinched and was led away.

As Lucas walked out of the courtroom, Father Messmer hurried to him. "I must talk with you. Herr Klaus Teuber is trying to reach you. He said it's urgent."

33

Father Messmer drove Lucas in silence to the Teuber home. Drained by the mission to capture Kaltenbrunner, Lucas imagined countless scenarios to account for the sudden summons from Erika's father: Was she lost? Injured? Dead? He tried to fight away hope that she'd simply come home.

Father Messmer broke the silence. "Never lose your faith, my son."

"Do you know why he wants to see me?"

They stopped at the Teubers' gate, and Father Messmer handed Lucas the note the lady in black had given him.

"What's this?"

"Read it later. You should go in now."

Lucas raced through the gate and jumped onto the porch as Erika leaped through the door and flew into his arms. They kissed and cried for several moments. Lucas grasped her shoulders and gazed into her tired, happy eyes that seemed to drink him in. Wearing her blue and green dirndl skirt, she took his hand and placed it on the lump in her belly. "I'm so sorry, Lucas."

He covered her hand with his and felt the bracelet. He stepped back, gazed at her tears, and smiled. "I've dreamed so many times of touching your bracelet again."

"Can you ever forgive me?"

"Would you like to take a walk?"

"I would rather go inside."

"We have to talk about this. I cannot live with this child."

She jerked his hand. "Not now."

Ursula and Klaus Teuber came onto the porch and hugged them. They all cried happy tears. Pressing her apron against her thighs, Ursula said, "Are you hungry, Lucas?" She took his hand and led him into the kitchen. "Look, I made your favorite—apple strudel. Come, take your plate, and we will go into the salon. I will bring more for Eri and Klaus."

"I've never heard you call her Eri."

"Ah, we gave her a new name when she came home to a new life."

"How did she escape?"

Ursula held her index finger over pursed lips.

Lucas hugged her, and they walked into the salon.

Lucas paused, removed the note, read it, and slipped it back into his pocket.

Ursula smiled. "It's so wonderful to have our family together again."

Erika said, "Mutti, don't be presumptuous."

They laughed, and Klaus said to Lucas, "Can you talk about all that has happened to you?"

"Not now, but I have one question."

"Anything."

"Did the soldier that I stabbed in the mine survive?"

Klaus laced his fingers. "No. But the Nazis said he did and could identify his assailant."

Erika jumped up. "Come, Lucas. Walk with me."

They left and started along the trail leading toward the lake. Erika said, "Where would you like to go?"

He stopped and looked into her eyes. "May I call you Eri?"

"Yes, you know you can."

"Will you come with me to my mother's grave?"

She said nothing, but took his hand and began walking.

Bracing alpine winds swept across Altausseer See, flattening wildflowers and Erika's dirndl.

Lucas walked with her to a grassy knoll and stood by the solitary headstone. He touched the cold gray granite and read again the inscription: Gott Weiss Varum—God knows why.

Erika said, "Now, I will tell you what happened." She went through the public massacre, the family's capture, and Kaltenbrunner's heinous proposition, often pausing as her tears flooded down her face. "When he left Villa Kerry, his female guard brought me home. She had understood my plight and was sympathetic, when she could be. Kaltenbrunner was a monster: arrogant, sex-crazed, and demanding. Living with him made me want to die." She gazed into Lucas's eyes. "The only thing that kept me from killing myself was thinking of my parents and you . . . and of us."

"I've thought of you every day and night and tried to picture our life—together."

They sat in silence. Clouds covered the Loser's crown, and Lucas remembered the biplane crisis. His mind raced over the past months: his fright as he slammed the knife into Horst Schrader's chest, running for his life, the bone house, Ratwein, and all the rest. How must Erika have felt, living a nightmare? He couldn't imagine.

He eased his hand onto the lump in her belly. "Have you considered—"

"I will not kill this baby."

"I didn't mean that . . . an adoption."

"Lucas, you are asking me to choose between you and this child. If you cannot forget the devil that caused this and be this baby's father, then I must live without you."

"Never." He handed her the note. "Read this."

She read it, gasped, and looked up at him. "His wife wants to adopt this child." She nodded, wrapped him in her arms, and kissed him. "I love you."

Lucas smiled. "I would like to name our first boy for my father, Edouard."

END

ABOUT THE AUTHOR

Dr. Cy Vaughn was born in Longview, Texas and grew up in Lake Charles, Louisiana. After graduating from Louisiana State University School of Medicine, he trained in surgery in US public health service hospitals in New York, New Orleans, Phoenix, and at the University of Utah.

He is certified by the American Board of Surgery, the American Board of Thoracic and Cardiac Surgery, and is a member of the American Association for Thoracic Surgery and the European Association for Thoracic and Cardiac Surgery, among others.

During Dr. Vaughn's thirty-one years of practice in Phoenix, he performed numerous Arizona Surgical Firsts: Coronary Artery Bypass; Implantation of an Artificial Heart (The Phoenix Heart) to treat heart transplant rejection; and others. He has lectured in Phoenix, Vienna, Tokyo, London, Berlin, Zurich, and New York.

His writing career began with the publication of numerous cardiac and thoracic surgery articles. His first novel, *The Phoenix Heart*, is a fictional adaptation of his artificial heart implant to treat transplant rejection, a world first.

He recently signed a publishing contract with Wheatmark Publishing for *Depot Dora*, based on Operation Ebensburg, a World War II mission, the heroic story of an Austrian patriot who saved the world's largest cache of Nazi confiscated art from Depot Dora, Hitler's codename for the Austrian salt mine.

Cy has also written a collection of poems, *Listen*, and numerous songs.

Lightning Source UK Ltd.
Milton Keynes UK
UKOW02f1957300816

281860UK00004B/190/P